International Velvet

Best known for his direction of such compassionate films as *Whistle Down The Wind*, *The L-Shaped Room*, *The Whisperers*, *The Raging Moon* and *The Slipper And The Rose*, Bryan Forbes is also the author of two novels, a highly acclaimed volume of autobiography and, more recently, *Ned's Girl*, the biography of Dame Edith Evans.

He is married to Nanette Newman, herself a best-selling writer, and they have two daughters, Sarah and Emma, both now embarked on literary careers.

Bryan Forbes

International Velvet

Pan Books in association with
Heinemann

First published simultaneously 1978 by William Heinemann Ltd
and Pan Books Ltd,
Cavaye Place, London SW10 9PG
Copyright © 1978 by Metro–Goldwyn–Mayer Inc
ISBN 0 330 25593 2
Printed and bound in Great Britain by
Cox & Wyman Ltd, London, Reading and Fakenham

This novel and the screenplay from which it derives would not have been possible without the inspiration of Enid Bagnold's classic story *National Velvet*. The author would like to acknowledge his debt and, in homage, dedicate this sequel to Miss Bagnold, with love and admiration.

ONE

Today

The woman with the unexpected name walked along the edge of the sea at ebb tide under a sky the texture of greaseproof paper, her red trenchcoat the only stab of colour for miles. Behind her the ruffled sands of the estuary, dotted with dark wounds of seaweed, stretched back inland like a freckled, pointed hand.

The woman was forty or thereabouts (at any rate of an age when birthdays were no longer treasured), though there were few revealing clues in her face – certainly nothing that a stranger, coming upon her for the first time, could have discerned. She walked slowly, sometimes looking out to sea. A sudden lick of wind salted her lips and she turned from it. At that moment she saw a single horse and rider coming across the sands from the ruined coastguard cottages. Seagulls rose like soundless helicopters as the horse approached, hovered above, then settled again when the intruders had passed.

The woman watched and for a moment something approaching happiness changed her features: it was as if a verdict of guilty had suddenly been reversed. But the mood was short-lived – as horse and rider drew closer the smile that anticipated recognition died on her lips. The rider was a child, breathless, an inhabitant of that world that exists between exhilaration and danger, oblivious to all but the power of the animal beneath the saddle.

Velvet (for that was the woman's unexpected name) watched them for a few seconds more as they turned away from her in a wide arc, splashing through the shallow rock pools, sure-footed in a way she would never be. Then she resumed her slow, even walk. She thought, what a fool I was, how stupid of me, typically stupid of me, putting my one egg in my one basket. She mouthed the words, for there was nobody to hear, saying to herself, Love makes all the choices for us . . . the options are never open. And not for the first time that morning she had the feeling that everything was accelerating out of control.

Velvet's foot touched something pliant. She looked down. A dead sea bird lay at the water's edge, feathers matted with oil, the beak thrust into the damp sand. She shivered. A small wave washed over the dead bird, moving it gently, the neck elongated by the motion until edged back by the next wave. Velvet was a great believer in omens, and once again she took the folded telegram from her trenchcoat pocket and re-read the terse, impersonal message. GPO ALL PURPOSE TELEGRAM was the heading – bureaucracy never failed in these matters – and then the message itself: GETTING MARRIED ITS SILVER AND GOLD WISH ME LUCK LOVE SARAH. Ever since it had been delivered that morning she had tried to read happiness into it, but the words were coded for her, happiness had been blurred.

She left the beach and took the long route back to the house, keeping to the dank path that ran along their side of the estuary. As she turned the last corner she saw the old horse waiting for her in the paddock below the house; saw his head turning as he sensed her and he moved to shorten the distance between them. She took a wrinkled apple from her pocket and fed it to him, amazed, as always, by the softness of his nose. He nudged into her as the sweetness of the fruit edged to the bared gums, twisting his mouth into the semblance of a grin.

'That's all you love me for, isn't it?' she said. It was a morning for remembering love. Feeling the warmth of his neck beneath her hand, memory moved in a flash of colour to a day many years before when there had only been one problem left to solve. 'Did we ever win, Pie?' she asked. 'Did we ever win?'

The old horse followed her along the fence rail until he could go no further, and she walked on, through the slanted gate, into the walled garden. The air was so still she could hear the sound of the electric typewriter – like short bursts of machine gun fire – inspiration fired from the hip, he called it – before she saw his face on the other side of the study window. He didn't look up as she passed him and entered the house and he was still bent over the machine when she came into the study and removed the full ashtray from the desk and emptied it into a waste bin full of crumpled paper.

'You ought to have a window open,' she said.

It was only then that he noticed her. He flicked the switch on the machine and the room was unnaturally silent for a few seconds.

'Lack of air's good for inspiration. Restricts the blood supply to the brain, makes me less critical,' John said. His eyes scanned the top page of a pile of manuscript as he replied and, in contradiction to what he had just told her, he picked up a felt pen and made some minor correction.

Velvet had long since resigned herself to the state of his room. The act of creation in the midst of such chaos was beyond her comprehension, but earlier attempts on her part to introduce a measure of order had led to one of their few serious arguments.'I do have a system,' John had shouted,

9

'it just happens to be an untidy system. It may offend you, but it suits me.' His talents, which she recognized as considerable, extended to embrace a way of working that dismayed her. Her own life was so neatly pigeon-holed that an absence of order in others could produce actual physical pain. Lacking his central drive, his dedication to a single purpose, she found that she had to make a conscious effort to ignore the squalor of his desk, his written Tower of Babel as he liked to describe it, dominated as it was by a four-tiered in-and-out tray overflowing with odd scraps of paper. All this in such stark contrast to the serious work he produced: a full-length novel every eighteen months for the past six years – novels whose sales diminished as the reviews became more respectful, novels she found increasingly disturbing, searching out, as they did, aspects of the human condition that were beyond the evidence of her own life. She was amazed by him, sometimes bewildered by him, for it seemed that he deliberately withheld from her those parts of his intellect that he gave so willingly to others, to strangers – that army of anonymous readers who bought his books and then further confused his life by writing long letters (which he seldom answered) detailing how he had changed their lives. 'Why don't you change my life?' she had once said. 'You do it for others.' 'I have changed your life. I've made it more difficult for you' – that irritating, disarming, writer's logic, he could turn on like artificial sunlight, tanning her with flattery, so that their arguments, always one-sided, left her flattened and resentful for days.

That morning, the morning the telegram arrived from Sarah, the resentment was close to the surface. The fact that he could work, resume his disordered routine, appear to ignore the news the telegram had contained, baffled her. She felt the urge to ruffle his calm.

'How's it going?' she said.

'Three pages I fondly imagined were Nobel prize standard and which, having reread, I now think are the pits . . .' He made another correction, scoring through a line of typescript.

'You always think that.'

'I always think it for good reason. Are you going to hover? You've been wandering lonely as a cloud ever since breakfast.' Then the smile, the smile she feared because he used it with such blatant ruthlessness. 'I know what's really bothering you. You're still upset about Sarah's telegram, aren't you? Look, it doesn't say she's married. All it says is "getting married".'

'But where, when? I mean, she hardly knows him. We don't know him at all.'

'Well, we're not marrying him.'

'Why didn't she say anything before, warn us?'

'Youth is impetuous, etcetera . . . Darling, it's no good going on at me. She's over age, of sound mind as they say . . . though that may be stretching it a bit, nobody who gets married is of totally sound mind.'

'Oh, ha ha . . . It's different for you.'

'Why? Why is it different for me?'

'It just is. I wouldn't mind any of it, I'm happy for her if she's really set on this what-ever-his-name-is—'

'Scott.'

'But what I think is hurtful is that she didn't take the trouble to ring us, she just sent a telegram . . . It's as though we mean nothing to her – oh, it's different for you.'

'You keep saying that.'

'Well, it is. You've got other things, you've got your writing and—'

'Velvet, darling, what I've got is a stack of blank pages that have to be filled seven days a week. Some people call it work, some people call it a hobby, a few call it art, those critics who actually read further than the dust jacket blurb sometimes describe it as obscure and none of it has anything to do with what we're talking about. And I'm not being clever, I'm just being realistic. She didn't ring you, okay go ahead and ring her.'

'I did. She's left the last number she was at. And no forwarding address . . . Anyway, you're right as usual. She's decided and that's that . . . if you put me in a book, I'd be the conventional mother, wouldn't I? Reactions normal. Except that I'm not the mother, I'm not anything . . . I'll get you some fresh coffee.'

'Just had some. You can take the cup, though.'

'And leave you in peace.'

'I didn't say that.'

She moved to the door, skirting the piles of reference books, carefully avoiding his eyes, knowing that if he was nice to her she would give way to tears. He said again: 'Hey! I didn't say that. I didn't mean that.' But by then she was out in the hallway, safe from herself. Facing her on a table cluttered with vases of flowers was a photograph of Sarah as a child, as she was all those years ago – a slightly truculent face, unformed, vulnerable. Velvet stared at it. She thought: we weren't much use to her in the beginning. We were just two people, two strangers, who got in the way of her grief. I suppose, if I'm honest, we didn't care for her overmuch at the start. No, that's not true. I loved her, because she was my brother's child. I loved her, I felt for her, but I didn't like her. In the beginning there wasn't much *to* like . . .

TWO

Yesterday

For as long as Velvet could remember the Arrivals area in Terminal No. 3 at Heathrow had resembled a permanent monument to the British building industry. To the arriving and inevitably weary traveller she felt it must convey an immediate impression of a city under siege where the inhabitants were anything but friendly. I suppose I'm like the rest, she thought. I always travel hopefully, and I always hate arriving.

She stood amongst the usual, slightly anxious, slightly apathetic crowd waiting to greet those friends and relatives intrepid enough to believe what the airlines told them when touting for their patronage. They were all wedged between barriers outside the Customs Hall, their anxiety blunted by the fact that the windows to the hall were painted out, presumably to deny them the transient pleasure of witnessing the various permutations of guilt. From time to time, as though suddenly disgorged like prisoners from jail, bunches of passengers clutching all manner of plastic luggage would emerge with wary eyes (those who had lied their way through the Nothing To Declare section holding back their triumph until they reached the open air). Then the crowd on the other side of the barrier would shift uneasily, chauffeurs would hold name cards breast high and harried package-tour stewards began to move like trained sheep dogs, heading off their respective packs, snapping at heels, emphasizing to their charges that holidays were not undertaken for pleasure.

Velvet held up her own card whenever a child came into view. The words SARAH BROWN were written on it. After two hours of false alarms she felt like a beggar soliciting alms. Above her head the metal shutters on the Flight Information Board began to revolve wildly, as though out of control. Gradually the figures and words sorted themselves out and she was able to read that the New York flight she was waiting for was delayed. There was no estimated time of arrival to mitigate the bads news. As she turned out of the crowd and made her way back to the snack-bar area, her mind encompassed a gamut of disasters: the plane had not taken off, the plane had crashed, had been highjacked, diverted, turned back because of engine trouble, was circling overhead preparatory to an emergency landing, was even now plunging to earth, a spent rocket of smoke and flame.

John was half-hidden behind a crumpled copy of that day's *Guardian* when she arrived at their table. He claimed he only read it for the deliberate mistakes and the cross-word puzzle, but that particular morning he had read it from cover to cover, gaining, as he put it, a penetrating insight into those liberal attitudes which, in a single decade, had helped hasten England's moral decline. The table was littered with the indestructible plastic débris attendant on the indigestible plastic food that so enriches our current lifestyle. In desperation he had tried to consume a bread roll, a pat of butter wrapped in two layers of irremovable foil, washed down with a tepid brew known locally as coffee.

They were sharing their table with a young Asian family – man, wife and a small child in arms who, having

14

been breast-fed, was now being offered some glutinous substance taken from a tin.

Velvet eased her way into the remaining seat. 'Still delayed,' she said. 'You don't think anything's happened, do you?'

'Yes.'

'What?'

'The bloody thing's late, that's what's happened.'

He pushed a cup of the indeterminate liquid towards her. 'Is it tea or coffee?'

'Sold as coffee, could be tea, tastes like boiled essence of saddled leather.' He lit a cigarette.

'You were going to quit this morning,' Velvet said.

'Ah, yes. It's will-power that does it. I happen to have the will to change my mind. Vice improves me, I've decided.' Consumed with the guilt that is the cross most confirmed smokers are willing to bear, he stubbed the cigarette against the side of the plastic cup: the material scorched but did not ignite.

'I was also hoping to finish Chapter Seven this morning, but I didn't.'

'Darling,' Velvet said, 'you didn't *have* to come. I said I'd meet her on my own, I did say that, I did offer.'

'Oh, I'm not complaining. I've enjoyed myself. It isn't often I treat myself to three hours driving in heavy traffic, not to speak of two hours here gathering valuable copy. I always wanted to live abroad.'

Velvet grimaced, then smiled at the young Asian mother.

'How d'you think I ought to deal with all this?'

'Sarah, you mean?'

'Yes. Help me. Write some of your best dialogue. I don't know . . . I'm so hopeless at . . .' She fingered the card with the child's name written on it which lay between them on the ketchup-stained table. She thought, that's how it's

15

going to be, nothing's ever going to be the same again.

'The last time I saw her she wasn't much older than . . .' She inclined her head towards the Asian baby and smiled at its mother, but the smile was not returned. We can't communicate any more, she thought. Not with each other, not with strangers, we all exist in such hopeless isolation.

John abandoned his attempts to refold the *Guardian*. 'That was here, too, funnily enough.'

'What was?' he said, and she realized he hadn't been listening.

'When I last saw her. They were just leaving for the good, new life in Arizona.'

John leaned across the table. 'You worry too much. Children always cope with death.'

'In books, you mean?'

'No, I didn't mean that,' John said. 'They cope with it. You did. I did.'

'Cope' was such a British word, a panacea for food queues in the war, for strikes after the war. 'We coped,' people said proudly. The ship was sinking and the lifeboats were too rusty to launch, so we made a raft of compromises and we coped. But she couldn't remember a time when she had coped, the best she was capable of was to push the past to the back of her mind. And now this, the arrival of the child, her brother's child, Donald's child, poor, dead Donald. Sitting there with John still willing her to accept optimism, she had a sudden vivid picture of that last scene in the desert, seeing it all in slow motion, like an instant replay during a televised sporting event: Donald's car leaving the road and the bright splash of flame against the barren Arizona landscape as it disintegrated on impact, the two figures inside making soundless horror. She had never really known Donald's wife, even the expression 'sister-in-law' meant little and now (perhaps mercifully?)

16

she could not recall a face, it was as though the flames had obliterated memory as well as human flesh. In childhood Donald had exasperated her and she remembered that period of his life vividly, but of him as a man, a husband, a father, she had no recall. It's a fallacy, she thought, to think that families remain intact, sometimes we forget those closest to us more easily than we do strangers.

The effort of memory was so intense she didn't hear John talking to her, and he repeated his last statement. 'It's down, they've just announced it. Flight 510, isn't that the one?'

'Yes,' she said, 'when?'

'Just now, didn't you hear it?'

She was already on her feet, as though her urgency now could somehow make up the lost time. 'What's the panic?' John was saying as she threaded her way through the crowded tables. 'Even though it's landed, it'll still take an age. They've perfected the technique of delay.' But his cynicism that normally she found so amusing grated her and she ignored him, making her way past the crush of fellow sufferers, clutching the card in front of her so that those ahead gave way, behaving as people do when presented with anything slightly untoward.

It was another half an hour before the first passengers from Sarah's flight began to trickle through Customs. Velvet tried to compose herself, rehearsing her opening lines, rephrasing them, forgetting them. How do you talk to a bereaved child? she thought. Do you mention it, the unspeakable, or do you ignore it?

She managed to ease her way to the front of the barrier and was rewarded by having her bottom pinched by a bland, middle-aged man with pebble spectacles who seemed type-cast for an atom spy in some B movie. Velvet stepped heavily on his toes before turning to concentrate on the blurred faces now passing by in increasing numbers.

'Excuse me,' she said to a student, 'but could you tell me, were you on Flight 510?'

'510, yeah.'

It was then that she saw the child in the exit doorway of the Customs Hall. Just a flash, nothing more, because her view was obscured almost immediately, but she had caught a glimpse of a strained, somewhat surly face. When she next looked the child had gone and for a moment she thought she had imagined the whole thing. The crowd cleared again and now the child was much nearer, walking without purpose, trailing an airline bag in one hand, the other hand clutching an ancient Snoopy. She was taller than Velvet had expected. Her hair was scraped back and tied in two spiky bunches. She looked straight at Velvet without recognition, a vacant, lost look, the mouth pursed as though concealing something.

Velvet waved the name card at her, and the movement attracted the child's attention.

'Sarah?' Velvet mouthed the words as she was jostled from her position by the barrier. 'Are you Sarah?'

The child stood like an island in the crowd, staring, just staring. There was nothing in the face, not pleasure, not relief. It was as though she was willing to accept anything at the end of such a journey.

Velvet repeated the question, saying the words now, and when she had just about convinced herself that she had picked the wrong child, Sarah nodded, then walked slowly to Velvet.

'Hello, darling, I'm so glad you're down safely at last. How was your flight, was it awful? You must be worn out. It's so lovely to see you.'

She put her arms round the child and kissed her, but Sarah did not react, it was like kissing a statue.

'I didn't want to come here,' Sarah said.

It was said as a flat statement of fact. When she spoke Velvet saw that she had metal braces on her teeth. I mustn't answer that, Velvet thought. Ignore it, that's the safest thing. 'Let me take your things,' she said, but the child did not relinquish the airline bag, and once again she forced herself to remain calm, kept her voice level, allowed nothing to show on her face. 'Uncle John's waiting for us over there, let's go and meet him, shall we? Where's the rest of your baggage?'

They found the porter with the baggage and made their way back to John. Once again the first meeting was a disaster, with John trying too hard and failing miserably, the adults both lost, fumbling for the right things to say and the child making no attempt to ease the situation. It was almost as if she had decided to ignore their presence: having made the original statement she appeared to have no further interest in the proceedings. Lacking Velvet's emotional ties, John could view the scene dispassionately and with his writer's eye he saw them as three characters on a bare stage, two of them acting out a play that the third had refused to learn, leaving Velvet and him to speak all the dialogue, give and answer the cues, fill in all the pauses.

They walked in silence to the multiple car park, took the graffiti-savaged elevator to their floor; walked in silence across the petrified forest of raw concrete to where the car was parked. Sarah looked on while her baggage was loaded and asked where she would like to sit, the front or the back, merely shrugged, looking past them, past their questioning faces – again as if they didn't exist, as if the world they had forced her to enter could only be tolerated if she refused to recognize any landmarks.

Because of the delayed arrival they were forced to drive home in the rush hour traffic: that and the inevitable road works that were a perpetual feature of every approach to or exit from London ensured that progress was slow. Velvet made several attempts to coax the child from her shell, making every excuse to herself ('she's still in shock'), concentrating on keeping her voice calm ('after all we are total strangers'), fighting her mounting panic ('remember she's just buried her mother and father'), being unnaturally bright at all costs. They finally gained the motorway and headed West, leaving behind the monotony of the urban sprawl, John now driving faster than the legal limit and for once she didn't back-seat drive, the presence of the child obliterating everything else in her mind.

'All your other things got here safely – they came yesterday . . . I unpacked them for you and put them in your room, so you'd feel more at home.'

At the word 'home' Sarah looked away. She still clutched the Snoopy, holding it round the torso, tightly, so that her knuckles were as white as the fabric of the doll.

'Uncle John put up some posters and pictures. I think you'll like your room.'

Still looking away so that all Velvet can see was a reflection of a strained little face against the dark green of passing trees and hedges, Sarah said: 'He's not my uncle. You're not married to him.'

'No, that's quite right,' Velvet said carefully. 'Well, you can just call him John if you like.'

John lit another cigarette. 'Or Mr Seaton,' he said. 'Whichever you prefer.'

THREE

The house at Mothecombe had originally been part of a large estate, but death duties had ensured, as in so many other cases, that the estate was fragmented – sold off piece by piece in an attempt to keep the main house, which had been in the same family since the time of Elizabeth the First, intact for another generation. Before John and Velvet occupied it, it had been rented out for a few months at a time to holiday-makers. They had taken it themselves for just that purpose, a place to escape to during the early days of their relationship, somewhere isolated and peaceful where John could complete a long-overdue book. It was very much a writer's house, neglected, anonymous with few distractions other than the distant cries of seabirds on the estuary. They had extended the first lease and then, as they acquired more and more possessions, so the house began to possess them. Unlike Velvet, John had a horror of putting down permanent roots, so he resisted the temptation to buy the house, preferring to lease it, although as the years went by and their arguments about the economic stupidity of such an arrangement became more frequent (Velvet needing something she could call her own), he began to have second thoughts. The fear of permanence fought with a writer's need for domestic peace, since despite all their protestations to the contrary, writers are creatures of habit: the favourite pen dipped in the same inkwell, the ancient typewriter that no secretary would tolerate, the ruined chair that nobody must repair or replace, for it is only by routine that originality flourishes over a long period, and those who live by the written word guard their routines against all comers.

It was a comfortable house, solidly built from local Devon stone, made to withstand the winter gales that moulded the tall Scotch firs surrounding it into shapes reminiscent of Rackham. The countryside around was full of legends, lying close to the borders of Dartmoor. It was a house that gave comfort when the fogs closed in, a house that changed and adapted to the seasons, now full of sunlight and the sound of bees when summer came, now scented with pine sap from the log fires when rain obliterated the view of the estuary. They had grown used to it, become inured to its defects, for what the purse cannot afford the eye often chooses to ignore.

It was situated a few miles from the village of Mothecombe and the approach road was rutted and badly in need of repair. Sarah's first glimpse of the house was in autumn; the garden, not yet stripped of leaves, had an air of neglect; dampness was in the air. As they stretched themselves after the long journey Velvet found herself looking at the scene through the child's eyes. She imagined the contrast between this – dank, mildewy scent of rotten vegetation, the mud flats of the estuary beyond – and the Western-film-like starkness of the Arizona desert (for such she imagined it to be, having never been there) which had been the child's only previous home. She had to stifle the urge to apologize for the house. It's only the beginning, she thought, I musn't panic, I must make allowances for her, forget what happened at the airport, what she said, how she said it. I have to make the effort now. And she despised herself for letting the word John had used seep into her brain. Cope, she thought, you have to cope, boring though that is.

But even as she made the decision she was given another glimpse of things to come. While John unloaded the baggage, she took Sarah by the hand and guided her through the archway into the sloping walled garden.

'The sea's just down there, just round the point. Did you ever go to the sea, or was it too far away? . . . I expect everywhere in America's a long way from everywhere, isn't it?'

The child didn't respond, but the uneasiness that Velvet felt, the sense of being at a disadvantage, was temporarily stemmed by the appearance of her dog, a Yorkshire terrier who had gone engagingly wrong somewhere along the line. She had bought him on impulse one afternoon, shopping in Harrods on a day-trip to London. He had been the last one in the cage, a puny bundle of saleable pathos, his coat wet from the heat or worse, indifferent to the many fingers that poked at him through the bars. But first impressions had been deceptive: within a few weeks of being brought back to Mothecombe he had grown in all directions, developing in the process a comic personality which ensured a slavish devotion from John that according to Velvet bordered on the nauseating. He was certainly a dog with character and that afternoon, standing in the walled garden with the alienated child, Velvet welcomed his sudden appearance as a desperate poker player welcomes a face picture card.

'Look who's here! The great Fred, come to greet you. Hello, boy. Say hello to Sarah.'

Fred did not go out of his way to make friends, being a dog not given to instant opinions: strangers had to be weighed carefully. Despite his inoffensive appearance and the characteristics normal to his breed, Fred nurtured deep and lasting hatreds, being transformed in an instant from a dog-calendar pin-up to a clinical maniac at the approach of the newspaper-delivery boy.

'Oh, come on, Fred, don't be an idiot, say hello. He's just being stupid. D'you like dogs, Sarah?'

'Some. I had my own dog. They wouldn't let me bring him. Some cruddy rule.'

'Well, we'll get him over. It's only six months in quarantine, and you can always go and visit him.'

'No, I can't.'

'Yes, they let you see them, darling.'

'I gave him away.'

'Oh. That's different. Tell you what, Fred can be your dog. He'd like that.'

'I don't want another dog,' Sarah said. 'Not ever.'

She returned Velvet's cold stare without blinking.

'Let's go in and see your room,' Velvet said carefully. She led the way into the house and up to the small bedroom under the dormer roof she had prepared for the child. She and John had given the décor considerable thought, arguing violently as to the taste of a young girl, and the final result was a compromise between the trendy and the innocent. A hasty trip to London had resulted in some Laura Ashley wallpaper with matching bedspread and some posters of pop stars. As soon as Sarah's advance luggage arrived they had tried to arrange her possesions decoratively. Not that there was a great deal to arrange and more than once Velvet found herself amazed by the rag-bag selection, alien objects from another culture that evoked no echoes of her own childhood.

Now, she stood to one side and watched Sarah's face as the child looked around for the first time.

'I hope you like it.'

'It's okay.'

'D'you want me to show you where I put all your other things?'

'No.'

'I don't know what you like reading, but John bought you some books and put those posters up.' She indicated some Osmonds, souvenirs she had found in Carnaby Street in a shop that seemed to sell nothing but T-shirts with pornographic inscriptions on them.

'Nobody listens to them any more,' Sarah said. 'They're really naff.'

I mustn't react, Velvet thought. Anyway, what does 'naff' mean? If I say anything now I shall undoubtedly regret it. I already regret it. She was conscious that the room was not a success, that all their well-intentioned efforts had been in vain, that they had guessed wrong. Well, we tried, she thought: it isn't our fault.

She had prepared hamburgers for a welcoming meal, but even these did nothing to ease the underlying tension and the only one who benefited from the experiment was Fred who found himself unexpectedly rewarded with an extra plate of scraps – an indulgence which promptly made him sick.

The first few days after the child's arrival were a nightmare. She slept a great deal of the time, so much so that Velvet rang the local doctor. It was, they decided, a combination of jet-lag and grief and they duly made allowances. John found his normal work schedule impossible, and they both lived in a state of armed truce with each other, carefully skirting round the edges of the dilemma. When she wasn't sleeping, Sarah made little effort to communicate; any attempt to draw her out proved exhaustingly abortive.

Arrangements had to be made for her schooling and

Velvet made several visits to the local village school to prime the staff there as to what to expect. None of the warnings she gave to others prepared her for what happened on the actual day.

'I'm not going to that school,' Sarah said when Velvet woke her on that first morning.

'Which school are you going to then?' Velvet said, humouring her.

'None.'

'Oh, that's just silly. You'll like it once you've got used to it and made some friends. Come on, up you get. I've made you a real American breakfast. Waffles and maple syrup. I got them specially.'

She pulled back the bedcovers and found that the child was already fully dressed in the same clothes she had arrived in.

'Those are funny pyjamas.'

'If you make me go to school, I'll run away.'

'I did that,' Velvet said. 'Running away is boring. I'll give you a tip, though – never run away on an empty stomach. So come and have your breakfast first.'

'I mean it.'

'I believe you. But you have to plan escapes. My mistake was I never planned anything. I never had any money.'

'I've got money. Real money. American money.'

She unclenched one fist and Velvet saw that she was holding some crumpled dollar bills.

'Right. You've got money, you're going to have your breakfast before you start . . . now, where're you running away to?'

'Home,' the child said. And for the first time her face mirrored what she was feeling. Tears ran down her cheeks and as she licked them away, the ugly metal brace on her teeth she was always at some pains to conceal, caught the light. For some reason this, rather than the tears themselves, touched Velvet.

'Now come on, darling. We're both being silly. You're not really going to run away, because I won't let you . . . I won't let you because I love you and this is your home now.'

She sat on the side of the bed and the child leaned into her, and gradually the tears subsided. Later she was able to dress her in the regulation school uniform and they went down to breakfast as though nothing had happened.

It was a false calm though, for there was another scene by the school gates, and it wasn't until the headmistress herself put in an appearance that Sarah allowed herself to be led inside. Not unnaturally she was the object of much curiosity from the local children, for few of them had ever ventured far from the village and the introduction of an American child had been anticipated with that mixture of wonder and envy peculiar to the young.

Likewise the unthinking cruelty of some children towards strangers in their midst was not slow to surface. During the mid-morning break period Sarah was singled out by one of the more persistent groups of bullies, led by a boy roughly her same age called Alan Wilson. They found her sitting by herself on the steps by the side of the outside lavatories. She looked up to find she was surrounded by jeering faces. Wilson suddenly produced an object from behind his back.

'Hey, Braces,' he said. 'We've got a present for you. Present from America.'

To the scarcely controlled amusement of his cronies of both sexes, he pushed a flat tobacco tin towards her. Before she knew what was happening he removed the lid of the tin to reveal what appeared to be a bloody, severed human finger. It was an old schoolboy trick, achieved by the simple procedure of making a hole in the bottom of the tin, through which the prankster pushed his middle finger – suitably daubed with red ink and bedded on cotton wool it produced a revolting and authentic mutilation.

Sarah's reaction was one of frightened revulsion: she was the model victim.

'Dead G.I.'s finger,' Wilson said with relish. 'All the way from Vietnam.'

Sarah backed up the stone steps, then turned and ran, climbing the school fence and disappearing across the field on the other side. Behind her Wilson and his companions fell about, delighted at such a complete success.

Sarah was not found until nightfall, a county-wide police search having been set into motion as soon as her absence had been reported. She was picked up on a main road attempting to hitch-hike, having covered some ten miles across country. By that time, of course, both Velvet and John had convinced themselves she was dead; either drowned (one of the first things the police did was to drag the nearby lake) or worse.

'It's always a relief when you find them quickly,' the local policeman said when she was safely back in her own bed. 'Quickly and alive, that's what I always say, Mr Seaton.'

'Yes, thank you, George,' John said, 'we're most grateful.'

'Pleasure. It's the other calls I don't like making. Especially when it's a child. I can do without them.'

As John said goodnight and closed the door Velvet joined him in the hallway.

'She's finally in bed and asleep. Exhausted.'

'Not the only one,' John said. 'Did she say why she did it?'

'No. All she said was she'll do it again.'

'Oh, great! That's something to look forward to. Let's have a drink.'

He poured them both generous tots and downed his immediately. 'George told me she got as far as the Langham crossroad. That's over ten miles, you know. A lorry driver spotted her first and then told the police. Gives you nightmares when you think . . . What've we let ourselves in for?'

'What've I let you in for, you mean. Did you ring the headmistress?'

'Yes. Relieved, but distinctly frosty. We had the statutory anti-American speech, then the standard bit about "some people" don't understand children . . . I always thought she was a bigoted, miserable cow.'

'You've never met her.'

'Yes, I have. I judged the Essay competition last year. She didn't agree with my first choice, remember?'

'I wish to God,' Velvet said, 'that people would mind their own business.'

'Or were you going to say, I wish to God we were married?'

'No. I wasn't going to say that.'

'Makes a change.'

'You can be so bloody hurtful, can't you?'

'I wasn't getting at you. I just meant that our situation's got nothing to do with that child running away. But you take it any way you like. Whatever I say you usually turn it around.'

She didn't answer him, but left the room. After finishing his second drink the anger which had been prompted by relief drained from him. He switched out all the lights and went upstairs to their bedroom. Velvet was sitting on the edge of the bed. He put his arms round her, but she did not respond.

'I'm sorry,' he said. 'You're quite right, I'm an evil sod at times – most times. It's just that somebody has to tell you not to take everything so personally . . . She wasn't running away from us.'

'Don't shout, she'll hear you.'

'I wasn't shouting . . . She wasn't,' he went on more gently, 'I repeat, running away from us, our situation. She doesn't *know* our situation. She was just running. Look, her parents are dead, killed in horrifying circumstances, she's shipped off to a strange country, meets an aunt she doesn't know and an uncle who isn't her uncle, dumped in some bloody awful school . . . Right? Well, then?'

'I know all that . . . but why can't I talk to her? I hear myself saying things and they're all the wrong things, and I don't have any patience. She's my brother's child and I know nothing about her.'

'Well, that's not your fault! She lived in Arizona, for God's sake! Why should you know anything about her? You've lived with me for six years and you know precious little about me.'

'Except that you're a miserable sod and you're always right . . .'

'Exactly, I'm a miserable sod, and I smoke too much, and I've got a hang-up about marriage, and I love you very much . . . and we'll live through it. Wait a minute, I hope we live through it, because I'm also a potential pyromaniac – I left a cigarette burning downstairs. Give me a kiss before we burn to death.'

'Look,' he said, as he started to leave the room, 'leave child psychology to me. I'll make a brilliant effort tomorrow.'

FOUR

'You really are dreadful,' Velvet said. 'Just like Daddy used to be.'

'What?'

John's innocence was mistimed and he knew it.

'You complain when the dog begs at meal times, then go and feed him yourself.'

'Did I? Must have been subconscious.'

He pulled a face at Sarah, soliciting her complicity. Breakfast up to that point had been a strained affair, with John and Velvet both talking at once, making small talk which fooled nobody. Velvet was reminded by the incident with Fred of a happier home and happier times: Donald, Sarah's dead father, as a little boy, always a menace at the table, spilling things, always poised on the edge of being sick, and glorying in it; she and her sisters tolerating him, coming to terms with the various revolting insects he kept in jam jars – her own parents calmer, with none of the histrionics that she and John indulged in. She remembered her mother, able to find time in the midst of chaos to counsel and console them all. Looking back it seemed that she had never once lost her temper with them. And her father, she saw him now sitting at the head of the table, a slightly Dickensian figure, looking at them all over the tops of his spectacles. Every time she went into a supermarket she remembered the scent of their own butcher's shop, a scent difficult to define – a cold perfume, not altogether unpleasant, compounded from sawdust and blood, which lingered on her father's clothes. The meat had been freshly slaughtered in those days, home-cured as they used to say and it was funny that with the family love of animals they had never connected the death of animals they ate with the others they kept as pets. One doesn't, she thought (although she suddenly recalled that Donald had periodically announced his conversion to vegetarianism, bouts of self-righteousness that seldom survived more than a few meals, for the smell of fresh bacon sizzling as they came down to breakfast was usually enough to make him renounce the new faith). She had often thought about the different layers of death, the fascination it holds for the young – something remote, something that happens to others but never touches the immediate family circle. Living in the country, it could be made into a ritual game. Your father was a butcher, but you didn't connect him with slaughter. He went to the shop and chopped up things, just as other fathers went off to banks and offices and performed equally mundane tasks. But the discovery of a dead animal on the road – a squirrel or a toad squashed paper-thin on the tarmac – that was different; awe-inspiring. She remembered the ritual mock-funerals they solemnly accorded to various tiny corpses, wrapping them in discarded boot boxes and burying them with honour and tears. Donald always insisted on reading his version of the Burial Service over the graves, lingering over the 'ashes to ashes' – a phrase he found particularly pleasing: that and the sprinkling of the earth. It hadn't seemed morbid then, such a preoccupation with death, and for a long time she had thought of it as something peculiar to them. It wasn't until she saw a French film called *Les Jeux Interdits* that she realized the game was universal.

'What's your favourite food, Sarah?' John was making another effort to break through the crust of resentment. This time he received a mumbled reply.

'I beg your pardon?'

'Peanut butter and jelly sandwiches.'

'How d'you keep the jelly in? Doesn't it slide out?'

'Jelly is what Americans call jam,' Velvet said. 'D'you hear that, Alice?' She addressed their daily help who had just come in with a fresh pot of coffee. 'We must put peanut jelly . . .'

'Peanut jelly?'

'I meant peanut butter and jelly . . . that is jam, on the shopping list. What sort of jelly, Sarah?'

'Grape.'

'Grape if they have it, Alice.'

She made a face at John. 'Sounds intriguing, doesn't it?'

'Sounds revolting to me,' he said, failing to pick up his cue. 'Is that very American? Probably why all Americans have rotten teeth.' Velvet gave him another, despairing look.

'You can talk. Most of his teeth are false, Sarah.'

'Capped, not false. I was deprived in my youth.'

'Deprived of tact, no doubt,' Velvet said.

But the sarcasm was lost on John. He had always found it difficult to concentrate on two topics at once, and when in the middle of a new book his vagueness often approached insanity. 'Are there some nice boys and girls in your class?' he asked. Sarah shook her head. 'There must be some. Did they talk to you yesterday?' Again the shake of the head. 'Nobody talked to you? Why was that?'

'I didn't talk to them.'

'Why? Not frightened, were you? That why you ran away?'

There was no response this time, so he persisted.

'Must have been something. Can't you tell me? I might be able to help.'

'He had a dead finger.'

'A what?'

'In a tin.'

'Who did, darling?' Velvet asked. Like John she was also out of her depth, for the dialogue had taken an incomprehensible turn.

'This boy.'

'Wait a minute,' John said. 'Tell me again. What did he have?'

'A dead finger.'

'I don't suppose it was a real dead finger,' Velvet said.

'Yes, it was.'

'Listen, if the child, if Sarah says she saw it—'

'Yes, all right, darling, I was only—'

'Can I just finish? I'll take her to school this morning and sort it out.'

'No, I don't want you to,' Sarah said.

'I'll talk to your teacher.'

'No.'

'Find out this boy's name. D'you know his name?'

'No.'

'Seems extraordinary to me.'

'I expect it was just a joke,' Velvet said. 'They always play jokes the first day, but it's never so bad after that. I bet you come home tonight and say you've got a friend.'

'I don't want any friends,' the child said. She got up and ran from the table. Fred followed her.

'Well,' John said, 'we handled that brilliantly, didn't we? Textbook Doctor Spock . . .'

It was quiet in the house. Early morning mist blanketed

even the sound of birds, and yet something woke Velvet. She sat up in bed, suddenly alert as we are when a reflex pulls us from a deep sleep. John, who had worked far into the night, stirred and then turned over onto his stomach. She waited for the sound to come again, searching to identify it, wondering if she had imagined it. But the waking premonition of danger remained, making her skin clammy and she slid from the bed and padded along the corridor. She listened again on the landing, then went and stood outside Sarah's door. Listened again, then tried the door handle gently, opened the door a fraction and looked inside. The room was empty.

She rushed back to her own room, calling as she went. 'John! Darling, wake up!' He peered at her without focusing while she grabbed some clothes and started to dress. 'Sarah's gone again. You ring the police and I'll get the car out.' He half-fell out of the bed reaching for the phone, knocking the instrument to the floor, and she heard him swear as she left the room again. Now Fred was barking. She picked up the wrong bunch of keys at first, and stumbled over the dog when she retraced her steps. 'Oh, get out of the way,' she said. 'Go back in your basket.'

Outside the premonition of danger seemed stronger; the very silence exaggerated the portents. She split a nail opening the garage door, swore, the pain swiftly forgotten, stored for later. The car started immediately, but then she stalled it, hitting the side of the garage door when eventually she got under way. Her headlights bounced back off the shifting pockets of mist, illuminating the hedges on either sides with shadows that rushed at her. Then no mist at all, a section of clear road and she accelerated too quickly, coming into the next misted area dangerously fast, half her mind trying to remember the

35

contours of the road ahead. She suddenly realized she had no plan, no idea where to look. The car left the road, hitting the grass verge, the steering wheel suddenly heavy in her hands and she saw blood trickling across the back of her hand from the torn nail. She braked to a halt and sat there, listening to the sound of her own heart. Then she got out of the car and walked a little way down the road calling Sarah's name, all reason suspended. It was then that she heard the sound of a horse galloping. She listened again, turning from side to side to track the sound to its source. Mysteriously, as though wheeled away, a section of mist shifted and she was given a glimpse of a distant hill, and on the skyline the black outline of a horse and rider. She ran towards it, the mist closing in again, a shapeless mass, alive, shafted now by the rising sun. Wet grass under her feet, she slid as she ran, not looking down, intent on keeping the compass of her mind fixed on that particular stretch of skyline. Sometimes she was blinded, running into sunlight, her lungs burning from the unaccustomed effort. She came to a barbed-wire fence strung with tufts of sheep wool, and ducked under this and a barb tore at her coat pocket. Now she was running up the hillside and once again, luck suddenly with her, the mists cleared again and she could see the horse and rider more clearly and closer. Relief fought with anger, the anger taking over as she recognized the horse as The Pie. Sarah was astride him, bareback, crouched low, riding as once, long ago, she had ridden and she felt a sudden rush of pain for the years the locusts had eaten.

'Sarah!' she screamed, still running, but her voice did not carry, and she changed direction, running at a diagonal to head them off. 'Sarah!' but there was no power in her voice. It was now that the child saw her and the old horse, sensing the familiar, slowed down. Velvet ran the last few yards and grabbed at the bridle.

'Get off!'

The child slid from the animal's sweaty back.

'You stupid little idiot, what the hell d'you think you're doing?'

'Riding.'

The slap of Velvet's hand across her cheek was like a pistol shot, and the old horse backed off.

'Don't you cheek me. You don't ever ride him, you don't ever ride my horse without my permission, you understand?'

'What's so special about him?' She stood her ground, blinking away the tears. 'Just because he won some old race a hundred years ago.'

Velvet took her by the shoulders and swung her round.

'Now you listen to me . . . and listen very carefully, because I've just about had enough of you! I'm sorry for you, very sorry, because I know you're unhappy and you don't want to be here, but that doesn't give you the right to make everbody else's life a misery . . .'

She broke off to regain her breath and they both heard the sound of the approaching police car as it bumped over the grass at the bottom of the hill.

'That's because of you,' Velvet said, 'and that's the second time in forty-eight hours. The police have got something better to do, you know, than looking for silly little girls . . . And if you keep running away they'll send you to a special school and then you'll really have something to be unhappy about.'

She pulled the child's face around. 'Are you listening?' she bent to catch the answer. 'What?'

'I didn't run away this time.'

'How were we to know? What would you think if you were John and me? So I don't want to hear another word.

You just do as you're told from now on and learn to live with it.'

She moved down the hill towards the police. 'Everything all right, Mrs Brown?'

'George, I'm sorry. It was a mistake this time and I panicked, I'm afraid.'

'You're sure now?'

'Yes, I'm sorry.'

'I'll leave you to it, then.'

When the police had left she walked past the motionless child to where the old horse was gazing. There was heat in the sun now and steam rose from his coat. She stroked his strong neck; some of his calm passed to her and she was honest enough to recognize and acknowledge the true source of her previous anger. I was jealous of her, she thought, it wasn't just the running away. She made me think of things I thought I'd forgotten, made me think of the day I rode The Pie into history at Aintree, round that enormous course, believing in him, knowing he could do it. We won the Grand National, he and I, and I was hardly older than Sarah. Now it's all behind me, it's over . . . but for her it's just beginning.

The next day she decided the time had come for a change of tactics. Twenty minutes or so before school finished she walked down to the village with Fred. She didn't want Sarah to feel she was being watched so she kept out of sight when the children streamed out of the playground and followed Sarah at a distance, noting that she was still without friends. Sarah went the long way home, taking the footpath that led down to the beach. Velvet followed. The child lingered by the water's edge, trailing her school satchel in the wet sand, a forlorn and vulnerable figure silhouetted against the afternoon sun. Velvet crossed the beach and stood beside her. The child, although aware of her presence, said nothing.

'The tide comes in fast here,' Velvet volunteered. 'You have to be careful you don't get caught.' She kept her voice casual.

'My mother swam across there to France . . . Well, not just here, not from this beach, but at Dover, across the Dover Channel. She just dared herself and did it. Over twenty miles, and cold – the sea here is always cold. They have to smother you with thick grease, otherwise you'd freeze before you got to the other side.'

Out of the corner of her eye she saw that she had finally aroused a flicker of interest.

'How old was she?'

'Not very old. She won a hundred golden sovereigns, they'd be worth a lot of money today . . . But when I was about your age, she gave them to me so that The Pie could enter for The Grand National. Did Mummy and Daddy ever tell you about that?'

'You won, but you didn't get to keep the prize because you were a girl.'

There was a meanness to the way she said it, but Velvet refused to be thrown. 'It was a kind of winning, prizes aren't everything . . . Where did you learn to ride?'

'Home.'

'Did you have a horse of your own?'

'No.'

'Hey! What did I tell you – tide's on the turn, it's round our ankles already. Come on, we'd better get a move on.'

She went to take the child's hand, but Sarah shifted her satchel to the other side.

'I think old Pie rather enjoyed his jaunt last night . . . I don't ride him now. He was quite a character in his day, and I'll let you in on a secret, he's going to relive a bit of his notorious past in a few weeks' time. A very special occasion, so I have to get him really groomed and smart. Would you like to help me? We've got to make him look a very beautiful gentleman.'

'What for?'

'Ah, that's the secret.' They were in sight of the house by now, walking by the side of the estuary. 'We'll share looking after him. Would you like that?' Sarah didn't answer, but this time when Velvet reached to take her hand she offered no resistance. 'See, the reason I shouted at you, the reason I was so cross . . . Well, grown-ups often get cross when they're scared, and you can't get scared if you don't care about somebody . . . I know you won't believe me, but I need you, just like your Mummy and Daddy needed you.'

The child pulled her hand away and turned to face her. 'They didn't.'

'Oh, 'course they did.'

'They didn't. They didn't need me. They didn't need anybody.'

'Why d'you say that?'

' 'Cos they didn't. They never did. I was always in the way, that's why they always left me.'

'Left you? Oh, Sarah darling, that's not true, I'm sure that's not true.'

'It is. You didn't know them . . . He wasn't your father, he was just your brother.'

She walked away quickly, passing Pie where he stood waiting by the broken fence. The logic of her parting remark defeated Velvet; there was no answer to it, no answer that she could find in time. She said as much to John that night when, with Sarah safely in bed, they discussed the latest developments.

'You have to be kidding,' he said.

'You may think that, but I really believe the only reason she's alive and they're dead is they never took her on that last trip. From what she told me they never took her anywhere.'

'Well, I suppose there's a kind of poetic justice in that. I wouldn't have written it that way, of course. In my books children always love their parents. That's probably why they don't sell.'

'But why didn't I know my own brother?'

'You did. He was just younger, that's all. People change.'

'What are we going to do?'

'I never take decisions,' he said, passing the buck. 'I only have theories about children, fictions. I can't relate to the real thing.'

'Well, neither can I.'

'But you will,' John said. 'That's the difference between us.'

She didn't believe him. Women are supposed to have instincts about these things, she thought. It was like learning a foreign language too late in life, a sort of penance, knowing that even if you mastered the grammar you were never going to travel and speak that language with the natives. Instincts. She willed them to come to her, blind her with sudden inspiration, but nothing happened – perhaps it was only mothers who had them? She remembered her own childhood, looking for past clues, thinking back to the time when she had been Sarah's age, recalling the fever and the fret, but the ultimate solution evaded her. Going to her room she opened a box she had not touched for years, and took from it some cardboard horses cut from magazines of long ago and carefully pasted on board to stiffen them. They had a sheen to them from constant handling. The memory of those days, the fantasies she had invented around the make-believe horses, crowded back and for a moment she could better understand Sarah's sense of being deprived. Then the comparison faded again, the link broke just as now the cardboard horses parted from each other – the paper made brittle with age – and she replaced them carefully in the box and closed the lid. Whatever else I missed later, she thought, I was never denied love and understanding then. She had a vision of her brother, changed out of all recognition, and that night in a confused dream she kept passing him at an airport; he stared at her like an enemy and then his face bubbled like plastic subjected to flame, becoming a distorted mask.

In the weeks that followed she never referred to Sarah's blurted statement. She made preparations for Christmas, challenging John's Scrooge-like distaste for such celebrations (in all the years they had been together they had never decorated a tree, but now, with a child in the house, she was determined to go the whole hog and she dragged John with her). During the evenings, with homework finished, she and Sarah made simple paper chains, painted fir cones she had collected, and the child began to catch some of her own excitement. Christmas in Arizona had never been an event, she gathered. She questioned Sarah and found herself amazed by some of the replies she received. She tried to reconcile Sarah's revelation that Donald, having become the complete expatriate, had frosted their desert home windows with the words HAPPY BIRTHDAY JESUS on one occasion. When in Arizona do as the Arizonans do, apparently. Listening to Sarah recount such events she realized how little she had understood her own brother. How odd, she thought, for Donald to renounce his past: at home, when we were children, the suspense during the weeks before Christmas had been unbearable, time passing in slow motion, every corner of the house a potential hiding place for gifts. They had prayed for snow, hugging themselves with delight when the temperature dropped and the skies were heavy. They had wanted the gift of nostalgia from the Magi, complete with all the trimmings. Donald had been part of all that, the season of goodwill had infected him with an uncharacteristic silence. She remembered one astounding exploit of her brother's, when he had removed the turkey from the larder on Christmas Eve and taken it to bed with him – the plump nude carcass lying beside him on the pillow, and his cry of anguish when his crime was discovered. 'Why do we have to kill things at Christmas?' he had shouted. Questioned further as to his reasons for such a bizarre episode he had insisted that he was trying to bring the turkey back to life. 'I could have warmed it up,' he said. 'It was nearly all right again.' How impossible to reconcile that tear-stained figure with the man he had become, the uncaring father in the alien surroundings of a foreign country. It was all very well for John to say people changed. People didn't change simply because we found out more about them – she refused to believe that.

In addition to the seasonal preparations, she also concealed – despite frequent bouts of questioning from Sarah – the secret concerning The Pie. The annual International Show Jumping Championships would take place in London a week or so before Christmas Day and the organizers had invited her to be their special guest of honour in order to mark The Pie's retirement. Having achieved the near-impossible task of keeping Sarah from the truth, she groomed the old horse every day, making sure that his coat gleamed with health, oiling his hooves, buying new ribbons for his plaited mane, combing and brushing him as though preparing him for a début rather than a farewell. 'And you're coming, too,' she told John. 'I don't want any of your usual arguments. You're to put on a suit and a happy face, and no grizzling' – talking to him as though he was the reluctant child. 'We have to make it an occasion.'

'Ridiculous.'

'What is?'

'Making all this fuss about a horse. Nobody's going to retire me from stud in public when my time comes.'

'You never know. Might attract a big crowd.'

'Well, I haven't got a suit.'

'Yes, you have, and I've had it cleaned. They ought to put a special warning on your cigarette packets: Smoking is injurious to your clothes.'

Somehow they managed to keep the secret intact until the actual day. Velvet went on ahead with Pie in the horse-box and John drove up with Sarah later in the afternoon. It was the first time Sarah had ever been to London and he went out of his way to show her the Christmas decorations in Oxford Street and Regent Street.

Arriving at the arena they were shown into reserved seats in the front row. John noticed that Sarah seemed to become a totally different child the moment the show started. She felt for his hand – an instinctive gesture – and held it tightly as the first horse entered the arena.

'Isn't it just beautiful!' she exclaimed. 'Imagine if you had a horse like that of your own.'

The preliminary rounds completed, the arena was cleared and the various jumps rearranged for the finals of the competition. It was during this interval that the house lights were lowered and a single arc light picked out the Master of Ceremonies in the centre of the arena. He carried a hand microphone and his voice was amplified through various hidden loud-speakers.

'My Lords, ladies and gentlemen . . . Before the final events I have an important announcement to make . . . and a very special ceremony to perform . . .'

'Oh, it's a pity Aunty Velvet's going to miss it all,' Sarah said, and John realized that she still didn't suspect the real reason for their visit.

'There are some of us present tonight,' the voice boomed, 'who will remember the year when the Grand National was won . . . decisively won . . . by a fourteen-year-old girl . . .'

John watched her closely, but the penny had still to drop.

'It was cause for celebration,' the Master of Ceremonies continued, 'and, alas, cause for disappointment, because although the young lady won fairly against all the odds, she was disqualified under the rules. But the fact is, rules or no rules, she and her equally remarkable horse, The Pie, were first past the post on that memorable occasion . . .'

At the mention of The Pie Sarah gave a shriek of excitement, causing heads to turn in her direction. 'It's her, isn't it, it's Velvet and The Pie? That was the secret.'

John nodded. For the first time since she had arrived in England he felt protective towards her. He gestured for her to be quieter and listen to the rest of the introduction.

'. . . I won't say how long ago it was, but tonight we are going to pay tribute to Velvet Brown – "National Velvet" as she was immediately nicknamed – pay tribute to her and to the horse she rode, for the time has come when The Pie is to be retired from stud . . . It comes to us all, but perhaps not so publicly or so pleasantly . . . My Lords, ladies and gentlemen, I ask you to show your appreciation as National Velvet leads The Pie on a last lap of honour!'

Now a dozen arc lights criss-crossed from high above Sarah's head, swirling towards the tented entrance and picking out Velvet and The Pie as she led him into the arena. They were greeted with a great burst of applause. The old horse was garlanded with flowers, his rug bearing the colours Velvet had worn on the day of their triumph. His ears came up as he sensed the occasion and he walked proudly round the edge of the arena, the applause consistently building. Now people started to get to their feet, hands held above their heads, and Sarah joined them, clapping louder than anybody. There were some amongst the audience who had been on the race-course at Aintree on the actual day and were not ashamed to feel tears on their cheeks, remembering the marvel of it, for the Grand National is a race that provokes extremes of emotion. They recalled the revelation of the young Velvet riding for dear life, winning the race as it was meant to be won, against all the odds, combining the beauty and grace of youth with the power and strength of a magnificent animal, both competing as one, horse and rider oblivious to danger, consumed with rare courage. They remembered, they shouted, they cried, and Sarah, caught up with the unexpected wonder of it all, shouted and clapped with them. She was still clapping when Velvet had left the arena and the arcs had dimmed, for the revelation had transformed her.

Later, on the return journey home, the excitement lingered like a sickness.

'You did win really, didn't you?'

'Yes,' Velvet said. 'I suppose I did in a way . . . we did, that is. It was all The Pie, really.'

'Will there ever be another horse like him?'

'There might . . . you never know, there just might be.'

She looked at John, wanting to share the moment, for that evening they had both, separately, come to the realization that by chance they had stumbled upon the answer.

With hindsight it seemed so simple, so obvious.

The child slept in Velvet's arms, her features wiped blank with contentment. Looking at her, Velvet framed the next questions to herself; it was as though in solving the mystery of Sarah she had left herself with no excuses. She sat very still as they drove through the night, her arm numb beneath the child's sleeping head, planning the next moves.

FIVE

Across the dark pastures and gentle hills, the only light
that overcast night came from a stable some half a mile
from the house. It was a cold March, with more than its
usual share of rain, rain that slanted low, driven by the
winds, so that those hardy enough to venture out had to dip
their heads against it.

Since the night of The Pie's retirement life with Sarah
had been easier. She was no longer the surly rebel and had
settled down at school and although still disinclined
to make friends of her own age and seemingly content to
remain aloof from any intimacy, she had drawn closer to
Velvet and John, accepting them as surrogate parents. Her
one obsession was the old horse; she spent long hours with
him in his winter stable, and was always first up in the
morning, scrambling through her breakfast in order to
have time with him before leaving for school.

Throughout the long winter Velvet had allowed the
scheme to take shape, discussing it with John when Sarah
was asleep, harking back to her own childhood longings for
a horse of her own and planning how best to spring the
eventual surprise. She was not by nature a patient woman
and as their relationship with the child thawed and
blossomed she found it more and more difficult to conceal
her plan.

On that particular March night she was waiting for a call from the nearby farm. There was a bay mare in foal, the last mare to be sired by The Pie, and the foaling was imminent. 'You can bet your life she'll drop it on the worst night of the year,' the farmer had said. 'And at no decent hour, either. They seem to like to get us out of bed. She ain't far off now. Over her time, you see, but then I like them a little over. If the foal comes too soon, there's a fair chance of infection. She's just about right, not too far over, but far enough to be on the safe side, the way I like it.' After two false alarms, he rang Velvet with the news that the brood mare had begun to sweat. 'I reckon this is it, Mrs Brown,' he said, 'so if you want to show your young lady what it's all about, like you said, you'd best get your face wet in the rain.'

'He thinks it's on the way,' Velvet said. John looked up from his typewriter.

'Well, don't tell me. I could faint just at the thought of it.'

'Aren't you coming with us?'

'Velvet, for the last time, if I set foot inside that stable and caught one glimpse of that amazing process known as birth, I should have to be put into intensive care.'

'You don't know what you're missing. As a writer you ought to be interested in all aspects of behaviour.'

She was busy gathering up coats and scarves as she talked.

'I'm interested in *human* behaviour. Very few horses buy my books.'

'You're just scared.'

'Yes.'

'Nothing to be scared about.'

'Listen, stop trying to convert me, just get Sarah up, otherwise you'll miss it.'

'I think you're mean.'

She went upstairs and roused Sarah from sleep. Since most children like nothing better than the unexpected, and since excitement in the middle of the night is an added bonus, Velvet had little difficulty persuading her to take part in the adventure. Bustling Sarah into warm clothes she rushed the amazed child downstairs and into the car.

'Whatever happens, just don't tell me,' were John's parting words.

The rain had eased slightly as they drew into the farm-yard and parked by the side of the foaling stable. It wasn't until they entered the stable and smelt the heady aroma of animal sweat and dung that Sarah became fully aware of the enormity of the mystery she was about to witness for the first time. She clutched Velvet's hand, feeling the heat of the stable rush to her cheeks and for a few seconds every-thing went out of focus and she saw nothing but jumbled shapes: the farmer and his stable-hand and the dark shape of the anxious mare.

'Won't be overlong now,' the farmer said.

He took a roll of bandage and started to wrap the mare's tail firmly at the base.

'Know why I'm doing this?' he said to Sarah. She shook her head. 'This is to keep her long hair out of the way, you see. Come on, my beauty, you get yourself settled down.'

The mare, who had submitted to the bandaging, now lay down on her left side, occasionally raising her right hind leg. She was sweating profusely now, her belly heaving as the contractions came and went at more frequent intervals. A sudden squall of rain lashed at the roof of the stable, like a signal, and at that moment the mare's waters broke. Sarah watched in total amazement as the gush of water splashed out, darkening the straw and soaking the farmer's trouser legs. Although she had questioned Velvet about the process of birth nothing had prepared her for the actual event. Her finger-nails razored into Velvet's palm, and she stood transfixed as two small, pale hoofs, wrapped in the amniotic sac, suddenly appeared in the birth channel.

The farmer and his helper moved swiftly, grabbing at the foal's hoofs, ripping the sack with controlled force and then the foal slipped out past the shoulders, the head tucked in between the forelegs. The mare's swollen belly heaved with the final contractions and the rest of the body slid on to the saturated bedding. The farmer tore away the rest of the sac and the foal flopped out, suddenly denuded of all security, separated at long last, after eleven months, from the only warmth it had ever known. It lay there breathing rapidly.

'Nice little colt,' the farmer said. 'A pretty little bay colt.'

He knelt by the foal and with the sudden movement the mare lifted her head to look back at the result of her labours. The farmer took the umbilical cord and pinched it between thumb and forefinger at a point a few inches from the foal's wet belly.

Sarah had scarcely recovered from the revelation of the birth when she saw the foal attempting to struggle to its feet. As he stepped back to give it room, the farmer glanced at her and smiled.

'What d'you think of that? That's instinct, that is, something that goes way back, before any of us were ever heard of. Back to the times when horses, wild horses, roamed all over the place in great herds. See, when the mares dropped them, on the plains like, not in a warm stable like this, they had to fight from the first moment, fight to get to their feet, fight to survive. Because there was always other animals skulking around, ready to pick off the weak ones. The herd had to be ready to move on at any moment, and if a foal couldn't follow, then he was a goner, see? And that's still with them, with that young fellow there. He don't know why, but something tells him he's got to get to his feet in a hurry. Evolution, you see. Do they teach you that in school? They don't teach this, do they? This ain't something you can imagine out of books, this is something you have to see with your own eyes.'

While he talked the foal was making slithery efforts to stand on its own feet. Next it was the mare's turn to stand and as she raised herself, the cord snapped and the farmer applied iodine to the short end still connected to the foal. The sac dangled below the mare's hindquarters as she moved to the foal and began to lick it dry. The foal fell down again, spindly legs flailing for purchase on the straw, then finally scrambled upright.

'Is it all right?' Sarah asked, finding her voice at last.

'Aye, nothing wrong with him. He's gonna be a good one.'

'How can you tell?'

'I can tell. He'll run, this one. He came from a good father, as I expect you know.'

'Yes,' Sarah said, feeling important, a friend of the family as it were.

'I was there that day, saw him win with this Miss Velvet riding him. 'Course none of us knew his jockey was a girl till after. Had us all fooled, she did, good and proper. A day to remember, that was. And now it comes down to this, like an inheritance, right down the line. Oh, he's a good 'un, you can depend on that.'

The foal was complaining for milk now, looking to suckle, and the mare allowed him to ruck under her belly, nosing her with a strength that a few minutes earlier seemed impossible. Velvet and Sarah stayed to watch until the farmer felt it wise for them to withdraw. 'She wants a bit quiet now,' he said, taking Sarah's hand in his own. 'We'll leave her alone, shall we, and go in and have a bit of breakfast to celebrate.'

He led the way into the farmhouse kitchen where his wife was already at work, preparing fresh eggs and bacon and slices of home-made bread dipped in the hot fat. There was hot tea served in brown, chipped mugs, the cream from the milk lying on the surface of the tea like small golden water-lily leaves. Sarah thought that nothing had ever tasted so good; the whole episode was like a dream and she knew that life would never be quite the same again.

'Could you call a horse Arizona Pie?' The question was Sarah's.

'If you wanted to,' Velvet replied.

'That's what I'd call him.' She willed Velvet to take more of an interest, since anything that diverted her attention from school homework would be welcomed, but Velvet remained bent over her own task. After a pause, Sarah tried again. 'D'you think – I expect he'd be very expensive, even if the man wanted to sell him, which I don't suppose he does . . .'

'Yes.'

Ever since the birth of the foal there had been only one topic of conversation with Sarah. She visited the farm every spare moment she had and had tried to make herself indispensable to the owner of the foal, volunteering for any menial task and performing it with a dedicated willingness that made him wish he had more like her. She saved enough pocket-money to buy a roll of film and borrowed John's camera, a complicated affair that he had never mastered and therefore could not instruct her in how to use, with the result that her snapshots were strange blurred images.

Artistic failures though they might be, she treated them with reverence, objects of undoubted beauty that, although not doing the foal justice, were nevertheless worthy expressions of her love. The hours she was forced to spend at school away from the foal were torture to her and she was forever being reprimanded for inattention, for in the middle of class her mind needed little prodding to wander and she could give herself up to the infinitely more rewarding reveries with which she surrounded the animal. He seemed to her to embody all that she had ever wanted, and faced with her total devotion he responded in kind, as animals will, so that the more she lavished her love on him the more he became a faultless god in her eyes. She had long since forgotten what life had been like before his entrance into the world.

'How expensive?' she persisted that evening.

'Oh, I don't know offhand,' Velvet replied, 'but a lot of money.'

'Yes. Because he's special, isn't he? Because The Pie was his father.'

'Yes. Look, finish your homework, young lady, otherwise you're going to be in trouble again in the morning. Have you got much more to do?'

'Only this rotten essay. Mrs Charles makes us write about such boring things.'

'What did she set you?'

'How I'd change the world and stuff like that.'

'Well, how would you change the world?'

'I wouldn't make children go to school for one thing. I'd let them look after horses and do all the things they like doing.'

'Why don't you write that?'

'You can't ever write real things, otherwise she gives you bad marks.'

54

'All right, but write something, because it's your bed-time.'

Later, when Velvet had tucked her in and kissed her goodnight, Sarah waited until she deemed it safe and then slipped out of bed to examine the contents of a tin box she kept under her clothes in the chest of drawers. It contained all her worldly wealth: the original dollars she had arrived with, two one pound notes and a collection of coins which swelled the total by another £1·78. She had no idea what a foal cost to buy and although on several occasions she had tried to get the farmer to name a price, he had always fobbed her off with some joking reference to millionaires. She contemplated the money, resigned to the fact that she would certainly need more than she had.

Immediately after her return from school the following afternoon she went to John's study. He was sitting at his desk, half-obscured, as usual, by a wreath of cigarette smoke.

'You busy?'

'Am I busy? No, I wouldn't say so. As a matter of fact I'm suffering from a bad attack of what is known as Writers' Block.'

'Oh. Is it painful?' Sarah asked.

'Very.'

'Can I get you an aspirin?'

'I don't somehow think an aspirin would cure it. You could get me an inspiration if you like.'

Sarah slipped her retainer off her teeth and slipped it into her pocket, giving John a conspiratorial look as she did so.

'It's okay, I won't give you away,' John said. 'What've you been up to today?'

'Nothing much. I wondered . . . Are there any jobs you'd like done?

'What sort of jobs?'

'Anything. I'm trying to earn some extra pocket money, you see. I mean, I could help you with your writer's thing, your block.'

'Well, that would be wonderful. How much do you charge?'

'I don't mind. I'd work for anything.'

'We have to have a fair price. What d'you think's the going rate? Twenty pence an hour?'

'Yes, that's great! I could get up early and do an hour before school and then another hour after my homework. And on weekends I could probably work most of the time.'

'Sounds a very good deal to me. I shall be able to retire When could you start?'

'Now.'

'Right, I tell you what . . . Writers' Block is very catching, so I don't think we'd better work in the same room. You go away and think of a story – could you do that?'

'Oh, yes.'

'Then, when you've thought of it, and written it down, you bring it back to me and if it becomes a best seller I'll double your wages. How does that sound?'

'Terrific! Thanks a lot, uncle John.'

She couldn't wait to get out of the room and find pencil and paper. Her head swam with ideas. What, during school hours, would have seemed an unbearable chore, now appeared to be pleasure undiluted. She had no qualms, it never occurred to her that she would fail to deliver the goods. All she could think of was that she had been given this marvellous opportunity to make a fortune and by so doing attain the thing she loved most in the world. With that energy that only the very young can squander, she began as she meant to continue, writing furiously, before classes, during classes (often being detected and reprimanded), after classes, in bed with the aid of a flashlight. She worked with the dedication of a Dickens or a Walter Scott, amazing John by the sheer volume of her output and more often than not by the audacity of her plots, which owed nothing to experience but a great deal to a fertile imagination. The closely written pages which she duly presented at frequent intervals had to be read when she was out of the room, for to tell the truth they were often unintentionally hilarious, and he had no wish to stem the flow or quench her enthusiasm. There were even times when he envied her capacity for outrageous invention and he certainly stood in awe of her dedication and industry. She delivered on time and was duly paid, the money immediately deposited in the tin box and frequently counted. Although Velvet was in on the plot, she assumed an air of innocence, for like John she had no intention of frustrating such single-minded purpose. They were both astounded by some of her fictions.

'Where does she get it from?' Velvet asked. 'Listen to this.'

'Which one's that?'

'Well, the last one she gave you, entitled "A Passionate Affair".'

'Yes, that's a beauty.'

'Whenever Julia came into the stable,' Velvet read aloud, 'the young groom felt his knees give way. He could see her heaving bosoms and knew that she wanted to marry him but could not say so because her father was a man of violent rages. So they panted at each other while they saddled the horse, and sometimes they held hands, but it wasn't the real thing.'

'Sounds like the real thing to me.'

He took the manuscript from her and stared at the

schoolgirl scrawl. 'I may have created a monster,' he said. 'Harold Robbins, eat your heart out!'

The day came when Sarah judged that she had saved enough. She took her tin box to school and immediately class was let out she ran all the way to the farm. Mr Curtis was working a tractor in one of the fields and she waved and shouted to attract his attention as she approached.

'Excuse me, excuse me!'

He cut the tractor engine and waited for her.

'I think I've got enough now.'

'How's that then?'

'I've been working, you see. Earning lots of money and I've saved it all.'

She took the lid off her tin box and showed him the contents. He studied it carefully.

'My word, yes,' he said, and she could see he was suitably impressed.

'So I've come to buy the foal, like you said. Is it enough?'

'Oh, I'd say that's enough all right, yes.' He looked away and felt in his torn pocket for a packet of cigarettes. 'Or it would have been, like.'

'Would have been?'

'Aye. He's been sold, you see.'

'Sold?'

'Aye. Somebody come and bought him only yesterday.'

For a moment Sarah couldn't see his face: it swam away from her and back again.

'But they can't have bought him,' she said. 'I've been saving up.'

'Yes, it's unfortunate, like. In the circumstances. But I

didn't know, you see. I didn't know you was so keen. Had I have known you was serious, like, I'd have waited. But I didn't have the knowledge of your bid.'

Cigarette smoke haloed around his head, and he looked past her as though ashamed of meeting her accusing eyes. 'Expensive things, foals,' he went on, using a quiet voice. 'Cost a lot to feed, so I had to take the first definite offer, you see. I'm really sorry, young lady, and that's the truth.'

Sarah stared at him, then put the lid back on her tin. She didn't want to cry in front of him. 'Was it a nice person who bought him?'

'Oh, I think so, yes. I wouldn't let him go anywhere nasty.'

She nodded. 'Well, thank you.' She turned away quickly. 'It's a real pity, that's for sure.' Mr Curtis said, as he watched her go.

The moment she was safely out of sight she allowed herself to cry. The injustice of it all was the hardest part to accept: the knowledge that all her plans had been pointless. She felt that she would never trust anybody ever again, that she had been singled out to be a loser all her life. The heaviness of the money in the tin box, so recently a comfort, now became the focus of all her hatred for the adult world. When she reached the path by the estuary she stumbled across the clumps of sharp reed grass until she was close to the water. Then she hurled the tin as far as she could. On the other side of the estuary a flock of gulls took to the air. The tin landed with a splash of rusty-coloured mud and was lost to sight.

John was waiting for her as she approached the house. 'Been looking for you,' he said. 'I thought your last story was a humdinger. Definitely worth a bonus. Here.' He held out a pound note. Sarah shook her head.

'It's too late.'

'Why? What's happened?'

She knew it would be a long time before she could talk about it to anybody. 'Nothing. Just something ... I don't want it any more.'

'But you earned it.'

'Doesn't matter.'

'Well, I'll keep it for you,' he said. 'Have you seen Velvet? She was looking for you too. I think's she's in the garden picking blackberries.'

Trailing her school satchel, Sarah went in search of Velvet. Fred came running to greet her, running with a sideways progression, like an aircraft drifting, that denoted his pleasure, but she had no time for him and he stopped, rebuffed, then assumed an air of indifference.

'Hallo, darling,' Velvet called. 'You're late today. Did they keep you in at school?'

'No.'

'You seem depressed about something. Are you?'

'Sort of.'

'Anything you want to tell me?'

Sarah didn't answer.

'Well, don't be depressed. Can't be that bad. Go and see old Pie. He'll cheer you up. I was looking for him just now, and couldn't see him, so he might have got out of the field. You know how he likes to wander if he gets half a chance. Go and see if you can find him for me.'

Sarah wandered off without enthusiasm: The Pie was too great a reminder of her own loss. She looked for him in the place where he usually stood at that time of day, then lifted her eyes to search further up the hillside. There was a horse on the skyline, but it seemed too small to be Pie. She stared hard; although it definitely wasn't Pie it seemed to be familiar. Turning back to shout to Velvet that they had a stray in the paddock, she saw that John and Velvet were hugging each other – the sort of embrace that people use when they are consumed with the excitement of good news. She looked again at the outline of the animal on the skyline and now as she stared the horse raised its head, as though aware of her presence below, and suddenly the pain she had carried for the last hour drained from her, to be replaced by a pain of another sort – that pleasurable agony that comes so rarely in life, the realization that complete happiness is still possible. It was the foal, *her* foal. And as she spun round and was confronted by the shared delight of Velvet and John, she could hardly balance herself.

'It is, isn't it?' she screamed. 'It's the foal, it's my foal. You bought him, it was you all the time!'

She did not hear their reply because she was running, down the bank, through brambles, jumping the ditch, then over the barbed wire fence without caution, and running on up the hill. And the foal, hearing her cries, loped towards her, then broke into a trot, ears up, and they met in the middle of the field like lovers. She flung her arms round his neck, pressing her face into unyielding warmth, and his head came round and he nosed her, staining her school dress with grass juice from his soft mouth. She kissed his neck, frenzied with joy, made mad suddenly, aware only of a sensation of weightlessness, as though ordinary life had stopped forever.

SIX

Sarah and the foal grew together. Watching them, Velvet couldn't help seeing bits of her own life more clearly, and sometimes it was as if past and present merged. How different, she thought, and yet how alike we are – both pulled by chance: the Pie coming to me because of a number picked out of a hat, changing my life forwards and backwards; Sarah drawn from Death's lottery and sent here, saddled with me and John as the confidential agents of her miseries and good fortunes, the choice made without reference to her; and now I have to urge history to repeat itself by buying the foal, starting the whole cycle over again, living my life through her. Was it her need or mine I satisfied?

She asked the question, but avoided the answer. Life now was too happy and calm to be challenged. It'll have to run its course now, she thought: love – or that aspect of love we are fearful of identifying too closely – makes the decision for us.

Gradually, imperceptibly, a change came over the whole household. John, who loved repetition, his only voyages of discovery confined to the fictions he invented at his desk, rediscovered his capacity to be startled and excited, becoming the complete, doting, surrogate father, prey to all those fears that make men a slave to their daughters.

He went to great lengths to conceal his sentimentality, assuming a casualness when challenged, but unable to keep the mask in place for long.

In Velvet's case the same emotions altered her in subtler ways. Echoes from the past came back distorted: *when you're older you'll see things differently* – but it wasn't true, not in her case. I see everything the same, she thought. The same mistakes, the same sense of life accelerating out of control. She tried to enter Sarah's life by the back door, a reluctant thief creeping in unobserved, wanting to share rather than steal. If detected, she retreated immediately and whereas the relationship between Sarah and John became casually intimate – 'laid back', in Sarah's favourite description – her own was more furtive. 'Help me,' she wanted to say, 'I need you more than you know,' but when she opened her mouth no sound came out.

The foal was duly christened Arizona Pie, his pedigree framed and placed in a position of honour in Sarah's room. She spent every spare moment with him, reserving for his exclusive use those stores of patience she denied to schoolwork. She had only one ambition and she pursued it like a politician: Arizona had to become the best horse in the world. All her pocket money went towards his comfort and towards buying every book about horses and equitation she could lay her hands on, and which she read and re-read until the pages was almost in tatters. She was willing to learn from Velvet, but could not tolerate any criticism of her idol: his virtues were obvious and his vices excusable. Every anecdote of his behaviour was recounted with a wealth of detail, time and time again, since in Sarah's eyes everything he did was special.

The only occasion when her idolatry faltered was when they began to break him in. Velvet tried to explain that because he had been made to feel so superior during his years of freedom, it was only natural that he would resent his introduction to discipline. 'He's just like you were,' she said. 'You were like that when you first came here, don't you remember?'

'I don't think I was like that. I mean, I had to do what I was told.'

'Well, he'll have to. But he won't do it right away any more than you did. See, he's been spoilt. He thinks he's the king, and now you want him to behave like everybody else. And he's a bit frightened, just like you, because it's all strange, different from anything he's known before.'

'But do you think he'll ever learn?'

'You did. But it took time. You had to be on a lunge rein, just like him. We gave you a little rope, then pulled you back, then a bit more and you didn't pull so much, and in the end you accepted it.'

Even Velvet had to admit that Arizona was more of a handful than she had anticipated. He had a will of his own, and since the most important thing with a young horse is never to break his spirit, they had to proceed with enormous patience. His introduction to the lunge rein was traumatic and it took them six weeks before he could be persuaded to circle quietly at a walk. After that it was a little easier, but he had such power, such self-determination that Sarah was often reduced to tears.

'You mustn't get depressed,' Velvet said after a particularly trying session. 'You see, he knows he's strong, stronger than you, but what a good rider has to do is convince him that strength isn't everything. It's your will against his, and once he's got it into his head that he's not going to get away with murder, then he'll accept that and make the best of it. I mean, he's a very determined horse. You've already convinced him he's something special.

64

Now you've got to persuade him that even though he's special, you're the boss.'

'Well, how will I do that? He always wants his own way.'

'Just think back. That's how you were. You didn't want to go to school either.'

After he had become reasonably responsive to a few basic commands, they introduced him to the roller, to get him accustomed to the feeling of a girth round his belly. This was not to his liking and again they had to endure his tantrums for a couple of weeks before taking the more difficult step of slipping a bit into his mouth. It was then, with that degree of unpredictability which so often confounds us in human as well as animal nature that he made the decision that surrender was the better part of valour. Much to their amazement he accepted the bit and later the saddle, without protest, almost as though he thought: well, I've had my fun, given them a run for their money, I suppose I'd better get down to the more serious matters now.

Most horses freeze when they first feel a rider's weight, but from the moment Sarah first got on his back Arizona seemed as eager to return her love as she was to give it. The impatience was now all his; it was as if he wanted to prove to Sarah that he was hers and hers alone and that together they could accomplish anything she demanded. For her part, Sarah was an instinctive rider. She had natural talent and found little difficulty in putting into practice the theory she had studied so eagerly; her only fault – as Velvet was quick to detect – that supreme confidence that the young come armed with, that cannot be challenged by the experience of others but only by the self experience that skirts the borders of tragedy. Remembering her own exploits, Velvet kept her fears hidden. Would I have listened at her age? she thought. Did I listen? No, of course not. Her mind went back to those halcyon days when she and

The Pie had roamed as free as Sarah and Arizona, when all she had asked of life was the chance to prove her belief in his invincibility. I'm here, she thought, it happened to me, you have to let others make their own mistakes and come out at the other end. She willed herself to remain calm, searching her memory for fragments of her mother's wisdom she could adapt to her own needs, but like shaken wine advice does not travel well through the years. She was proud of Sarah, for reflected glory throws a pleasing image and it was a period in her life when she felt curiously secure. The surface of their lives was unrippled; John completed a new novel and then, breaking new ground himself, attempted a biography of an obscure eighteenth century eccentric which, while not gracing the best seller lists, earned him a major literary prize and gave him quiet satisfaction.

Sarah and Arizona went from strength to strength. Her maturing control of the horse and his unswerving faith in her resulted in a partnership that outsiders, as well as Velvet, felt approached near perfection. Soon she was riding him at local gymkhanas, at all the small shows in the neighbourhood; wherever she could find a jumping competition or hunter trials within easy distance. In the somewhat closed society of the horse world their joint fame quickly spread beyond Mothecombe and Sarah was urged to enter Arizona in competitions further afield. This meant travelling expenses and it was John who provided the funds, using the money he had won from the biography. 'It's the first time I've ever put money on a horse,' he said.

As the years passed Sarah's bedroom walls became decorated with numerous cups and rosettes as she progressed from junior events to more demanding trials and although John's pride in her equalled Velvet's he was reluctant to leave his desk and venture out into the open fields to witness her triumphs. 'You keep bringing home the prizes,' he said. 'I don't have to be there. I know you're going to win and I might get corrupted, you see.'

'How d'you mean?' Sarah asked.

'Well, you know, perhaps I'm one of Nature's horsemen, and, you know, I don't want to steal your thunder. If they once got me on a horse, the others might just give up in sheer despair.'

'The conceit of the man,' Velvet said.

Then seeing Sarah's growing disappointment he allowed himself to be persuaded and accompanied Velvet to a Junior One Day Event which Sarah set great store by. He grumbled all the way there in the car, protesting that he was living on borrowed time. 'I shall have to work all night to catch up,' he said, 'otherwise I'll lose the flow.'

The weather on that particular day did nothing to improve his disgruntlement: it was bitterly cold, with a biting, rain-saturated wind that cut across the event field like gun-shot. He took an instant dislike to the other spectators. 'Are they real?' he whispered all too loudly to Velvet, 'or do they rent them?' He exaggerated his misery for the sake of effect, but naturally, like all writers, he was storing the experience for future use. Once embarked upon a particular mood he made a virtue of it in secret whilst continuing to present a different face to the rest of the world.

He watched a succession of young hopefuls complete the course with growing impatience and embarrassed Velvet by applauding in the wrong places.

'You don't clap until they've finished,' she told him. 'It disturbs the horses if you clap.'

'I'm only clapping to keep my hands warm. When's Sarah coming on?'

'After this rider. And this one's good.'

'Better than Sarah?'

'Well, as good.'

'Are we allowed to boo?'

She decided to ignore him. He fumbled with his camera, a seldom-used instrument he had brought for the occasion.

'Take the lens cap off,' Velvet said, as Sarah entered the starting box.

'Perfectionist,' he muttered. 'I can never see through these blessed things. All I ever do is photograph my own hands.'

'Excuse me, sir,' a voice said. 'I could take them for you, if you like. I'm quite good at photography.'

'Oh, fine, thank you.'

John handed the camera to a young man of Sarah's age who had been hovering near the back of their station wagon.

'You know who I was trying to aim at, do you?'

'Oh, yes, sir. Sarah Brown. I was at school with her. My name's Wilson, sir. Alan Wilson, she'd remember me, I'm sure.'

'Well, thank you very much, Alan.'

The boy handled the camera with a show of panache and commenced clicking the moment Sarah and Arizona took the first fence. Even John could not help noticing that she rode differently from the others. She made it all look effortless, keeping Arizona going smoothly and easily, and the young horse made light of the big fences. When he came to the wall he jumped it with feet to spare. John looked round to see if the other spectators were equally impressed, smiling so broadly at one woman who happened to catch his eye that she was persuaded his motives had nothing to do with the appreciation of good riding. He was just preparing to applaud wildly at what he was sure was going to be a faultless round when, to his horror and amazement, at the last fence Arizona brought down two poles.

'Oh dear, what a pity about that triple!' Velvet exclaimed. 'They were going so well – she had it in her pocket.'

'What happened then?'

'She just got too confident, thought she was home and dry, and relaxed. You can't relax in this sport. Not until you're back in the stable.'

'Does that mean she loses altogether?'

'Not altogether. She'll get a second.'

'Well, I think she rode better than the rest, certainly better than that fat girl. Didn't you think so, Alan?'

'I thought she was terrific, sir,' the boy said. He handed back the camera. 'I hope they come out all right.'

'Thank you very much.'

'Pleasure, sir.'

'Her first fan,' Velvet said as the boy walked away. 'Nice manners.'

'Yes, well, we always try and impress the parents, don't we? That's always the first move.'

'You are a cynic.'

'I'm a realist. She's nearly seventeen and very pretty. The next thing I'm going to have to buy is a shotgun.'

'You're talking like a jealous father.'

'All men are jealous fathers. Even those without children.'

'Is that a quote from something?'

'It is now.'

They joined the crowd in front of the Judges' tent to watch the presentation of the awards and afterwards went to the saddling enclosure to find Sarah. Alan Wilson was already with her, thus confirming John's worst suspicions.

'Hello, Sarah. I thought you were terrific. D'you remember me? I'm Alan Wilson, I once frightened the life out of you at school, remember? The dead G.I.'s finger. I borrowed your father's camera today and took pictures of you winning.'

'I didn't win,' Sarah said. 'I came second, and he's not my father.'

'Well done, darling,' Velvet said, as she and John joined them. 'Pity about the last fence.'

'I so wanted to win today. So he'd notice me.'

'Who?' John said, with another sidelong glance at Wilson.

'Captain Johnson.'

She indicated a middle-aged man standing with the judges. 'You know who he is, don't you? He trains the British Olympic team.'

'Well, I'm sure he did notice you.' She turned to the boy, sensing his agony at being dismissed, and smiled at him. 'We have to thank Alan for taking your photograph.'

'Pleasure.' He shifted his weight from one foot to the other; all his confidence had evaporated. 'I'll say goodbye then. Goodbye, sir. Goodbye, Sarah.'

She nodded at him, but her eyes were still on Johnson.

'He seems quite a nice boy,' Velvet said.

'Yes, he's all right. I just wish I'd done better.'

'I think perhaps, darling, you try too hard sometimes.' Sarah stared at her.

'You can't try *too* hard,' she said.

She might have been talking to a stranger.

'Well, for what it's worth, I was very impressed,' John said. 'I wouldn't go over one of those fences in a helicopter, let alone on those dinosaurs you lot ride.'

If he had expected to break Sarah's mood he was disappointed. The joke fell flat. A cold wind blew across the field, flapping the refreshment tents, and they stood there listening to the sound it made through the guy ropes, and to Velvet it sounded like a warning.

SEVEN

They were three rather ordinary young men, nothing special about them. One of them worked in the local bank, another was a car salesman and the third helped out in his father's grocery store. It was their habit to meet at the village pub every lunchtime and have a few beers and a sandwich. The eldest amongst them was also the proud possessor of a hotted-up Mini Minor, complete with racing tyres, double exhaust and trim. It would be untrue to paint them as villains, they were just ordinary and bored and anxious to prove themselves.

On this particular day they met as usual and Charlie, the owner of the Mini, had bought the first round. They were talking, as they always did, in exaggerated terms about their recent exploits with various girls. This was not only their favourite topic of conversation, it was their only topic, village life being what it is and young men being what they are. Their group on this day also included Alan Wilson. He was the outsider, tolerated if he bought a round of drinks, and the object of some derision: he was still at college, regarded by the others as somewhat dull, since the industry of others has often to be derided by those who lack the will to aim higher themselves. They were all discussing a recent film, a film notorious for its explicit sex, and Alan had been bold enough to admit that he had found it offensive and, what was worse in their eyes, boring, thus leaving himself wide open to a variety of jibes.

It was during this episode that Sarah rode by on Arizona. She had been exercising him on the common and was just returning home. It was no secret to Charlie and his companions that Alan was attracted to Miss Sarah Brown; his reticence whenever her name was mentioned was proof enough and the fact that he defended her against their more ribald comments brought in their verdict of guilty.

There is something about young girls on horses that brings out the worst in some people. Perhaps it is that nowadays owning or riding a horse is sufficiently out of the ordinary to immediately suggest privilege, and of course when this is combined with beauty it arouses in those who feel inadequate emotions that are both irrational and violent.

At seventeen, Sarah had matured into beauty, that combination of vulnerability and innocence which young men find most challenging. The way she sat on Arizona, the way she wore her clothes, disturbed them, and being disturbed they had to assert themselves arrogantly. They weren't vicious by nature, but the beer gave them Dutch courage, and the added presence of Alan ensured that on that particular day they went further than they had intended.

'Oh, I say, I say,' Charlie mimicked as she went by, 'it's the old Berkeley Hunt.' He affected an aristocratic drawl, which immediately reduced his two regular companions to hysterics. 'I say, darling, you've got a very good seat.'

Sarah ignored him, though at her first glance she had noted Alan Wilson's presence in the group.

'Hey, darling, I'm talking to you. You do know you've got a horse between your legs, don't you?'

'Leave her alone,' Alan said, 'she's all right.'

73

'She's a stuck-up little cow.'

What happened during the next ten or eleven minutes brought grief to three families, near tragedy to a fourth, and transient fame to a local newspaper reporter who, by pure chance rather than industry, was first on the scene.

Immediately following what Charlie felt to be a rejection of his wit and charm, he and his two companions drove off in the Mini, leaving Alan behind. They followed Sarah on her way home, overtaking her at speed, then reversing in front of her and driving back at her, forcing Arizona to rear up in fright. Sarah sensibly left the main road and took to a woodland path, hoping this would deter them, but again they followed. She put Arizona into a gallop and jumped a five-bar gate into a neighbour's field. Far from taking her to safety, it was the beginning of a nightmare.

Charlie and his two companions lifted the gate from its hinges and to Sarah's horror, drove the Mini into the field. Gunning the accelerator, they raced straight at her and Arizona across the bumpy grass. To them it was still a game, a good laugh, something to savour at a later date.

Sarah and Arizona had no difficulty in avoiding the first few passes, for the horse could change direction faster than the vehicle. She thought that they would abandon the chase after that, but they kept coming – Charlie spinning the wheel clockwise and anti-clockwise, rocking the small car into ever tighter turns in an effort to gain an edge. The gap between the car and the animal shortened and Sarah felt panic mount in the horse and smelt his fear. Sweat from his flanks soaked her riding breeches, and the effort of holding him tore at the muscles of her arms. For the first time she felt real fear and crouched low in the saddle to avoid the overhanging branches as she galloped Arizona in and out of some ancient oak trees.

Charlie anticipated her move and swung the car directly

in front of them: this time the gap could be measured in feet and Arizona jerked round, and she lost a stirrup. Changing direction again she headed for what she took to be a gap in the hedge. All too late she saw there was an iron railing at an angle across the gap. She tried to bring Arizona round, but by now he was too frenzied, he had committed himself to take the jump. He cleared it with ease, but she was unbalanced and was thrown as they went over, landing clear of the horse, but falling heavily, her riding hat spinning off, her head snapping back as she crumpled into the ground. She tasted earth in her mouth before losing consciousness.

Still on a high of excitement, Charlie failed to see a pile of logs in the Mini's path. The small car hit the obstacle, mounted it and turned over. For the last few seconds of life Charlie and his two friends saw everything in slow motion: an opaque nightmare of sky and grass as the windscreen clouded, then buckled outwards under the pressure of the contracting metal frame. The doors broke away. Charlie's hands, reddened with his own blood, clutched at the steering wheel embedded in his chest. The driving mirror flew backwards into the interior of the car, slicing the face of the boy sitting in the rear. Like some macabre mechanical toy, the Mini righted itself again, and with Charlie's lifeless foot jammed down on the accelerator, it raced around the field in diminishing circles until grass and mud acted as brakes on the twisted wheels. The screaming engine suddenly cut out. Disturbed crows took to the air with savage laments. Then there was a hiss of steam as the radiator burst, surging brown water over the hot engine and a second or two later the first flick of flame appeared. Mercifully the occupants of the car were unaware by this time, for the flames spread rapidly, licking backwards from the engine, engulfing the chassis, edging ever

75

nearer to the shattered petrol tank. The car exploded in a ball of flame, sending the circling crows higher, and burning débris fell through the branches of the oak trees.

The sound of the explosion penetrated Sarah's clouded brain, but it was just another noise added to the cacophony of the nightmare.

Lying in her own bed, secure in the sheet sandwich, she remembered some of it. She remembered the journey in the ambulance and faces peering down at her. Later she could recall saying 'Arizona' over and over again and Velvet sitting by her bed and holding her hand. She had suffered nothing more than a concussion and within a week she was allowed visitors. The first person to call was Alan Wilson.

'I got concussed once,' he said, in his usual shuffling fashion, for he was ill at ease, embarrassed at being left alone with her in such circumstances.

'Did you ever recover?'

The joke didn't register for a second or two. 'Oh, yes, I see . . . Yes, sort of, I suppose, you'd know better than me.' He was trying not to stare at her.

'I thought this might cheer you up, give you a laugh.'

He produced a square tobacco tin and offered it to her.

'That looks familiar,' Sarah said. 'You open it.'

'Oh, it's not that . . . I wouldn't do that again. I've stopped giving dead fingers.' He opened the tin: inside, lying on an envelope, was a single red rose.

'It's lovely, Alan, thank you.'

'There's a letter, too, which you can read when I've gone . . . Is there anything you want, anything I can bring you?'

Sarah shook her head. She stared at him.

'What happened – what happened to those boys in the car? Nobody will tell me.'

There is an honesty between the young, and he looked straight at her when he answered. 'They died,' he said.

She looked at him without expression. Then she turned her head away and began to cry silently.

'I wasn't supposed to tell you. Sarah, don't cry. Honestly, it wasn't your fault. Nobody thinks that. I mean, they were sort of my friends, and I knew what they were like. I wouldn't want you to think they were awful or anything like that, they just did stupid things. You mustn't blame yourself, you must just forget it. You're not frightened to ride again, are you? Because of what happened? You mustn't be.'

He waited. She still didn't turn to him. 'No,' she said finally, 'I'm going to ride again.'

There was another pause. 'Well, I'd better not outstay my welcome, I promised your aunt. You take care now. Don't forget to read the letter.'

He had no means of expressing the way he felt. The letter he had written, the letter she scarcely read, his embarrassed attempt to atone for his past awfulness by placing the rose in an identical tobacco tin, were the poor substitutes for love he laid at her feet. Face to face with her self-sufficiency – that effortlessly cruel self-sufficiency that young girls can command – he was at a loss to know what to do. Mumbling his goodbyes, waiting at the door for the reassurance that never came, he envied her the physical pain she had endured, for his own hurt could not be treated.

After he had gone Sarah fingered the rose: it symbolized nothing he had imagined, it merely brought part of the nightmare back to her, and she cried once again.

77

That summer held other sadness. Fred the dog died, quietly, unexpectedly, with nobody to see: animals manage their exits more tidily than human beings.

Sarah spent most of her time reading, for the house was full of books and she devoured them, often reading far into the hot nights. She became conscious of hidden meanings, of the ability of some authors to describe emotions that hitherto she had felt belonged only to herself. The moment she finished one, she hurried in search of another and it was during one of these excursions that she came upon a novel called *The Angry Victory*. It was with feeling of shock that she read the author's name: John Seaton. Although she was fully aware of John's daily occupation this was the first time she had been confronted with evidence that his labours at the typewriter had an end result.

She sat down and began to read. The fact that somebody she knew had actually sat down and written the words that now so engrossed her, filled her with a sense of wonder. It was as though some dark part of the universe had been suddenly illuminated. She could not put it down. But he couldn't have invented this, she thought, it must have all happened to him, it's too real to be a made-up story.

John came into the room unobserved and discovered her reading it.

'My God,' he said, 'where on earth did you find that. Didn't know I still had a copy. You know it was my first?'

'Your first?'

'Well, the first one that was published. Got terrific notices and sank like the proverbial stone.'

'Is it a true story?'

'Well, now, that's a good question. I wish you hadn't asked. Yes and no. Let's just say that the hero of the novel had sacred and profane traces of me in him . . . like egg on the side of the plate.'

'Were you ever in love like the man in the book?'

'Sort of.'

'Was it sad?'

'I thought so at the time. Then, years later I met the young lady again, who was no longer so young, and congratulated myself on my escape.'

'How did you meet Velvet?'

'We met – in the meat department of Harrods, a well known London romantic spot.'

'Did you propose to her?'

'In the meat department? No.'

'Anywhere?'

'You're getting better, aren't you? Doctor said you could go out tomorrow.'

'Did he say I could ride?' she asked eagerly.

'You know very well he didn't.'

'He's a bore! I have to ride soon. It's like a car . . .' she paused, as memory crowded back, and corrected herself, 'It's like a plane crash – pilots have to get back into the air as soon as possible.'

'You think so?'

'That's what it says in your book.'

'That book is a work of fiction. See, what you don't know is that I was a pilot in the war. And a lot of us crashed and some of us never wanted to fly again.'

'Were you, were you really?'

'Got you guessing, haven't I? See, part of being a good writer is never giving all the answers. It might not have been the meat department either. Could have been the pet shop.'

He smiled and left her to it.

With the resilience of the young, Sarah was back in the

saddle within a few weeks, and training hard. She and Arizona had now graduated to the top competitions and that summer proved to be their most successful yet. The partnership did not go unremarked. The selectors, always on the look-out for horses and riders talented enough to represent Britain in international events, had noted the exceptional promise of the young horse. Sarah's extreme youth raised question-marks in their minds, but they noted, conferred – and bided their time.

Alan Wilson refused to give up hope. He called most days, cycling from his home on the outskirts of the village, but it usually fell to Velvet to make some excuse on Sarah's behalf.

'If you don't want to see him,' Velvet told her, 'just put him out of his agony. I'm not always going to do your dirty work for you, you know.'

'Well, it's not my fault, is it? I didn't ask him to get a crush on me.'

'He's taking riding lessons now. So he told me today. Just to keep up with you, I suppose. I feel sorry for him, that's all.'

'I feel sorry for him, too, and I do want to see him, but not all the time . . . It's just that when I know I can take somebody for granted, I go off them. Weren't you ever like that?'

'Me? Oh, that was all a hundred years ago.'

'But you were like me, you told me, you told me you were only interested in The Pie. Why don't you ever ride any more?'

'It's the oldest reason in the world,' Velvet said. 'I lost my nerve. I was married by then . . .'

'You married?'

'Yes, and don't look so surprised.'

'But I thought you didn't believe in marriage?'

'I don't believe in some marriages.'

'So what happened?'

'I did a lot of things wrong, things I wish I hadn't done . . . Stupid things we all do when we want to hurt somebody, and I ended up a loser.'

'We were just talking about that,' Sarah said.

'Who?'

'John and me. Oh, not about you. Just things. Things like losing your nerve and all that. See, I don't think about it, I only think about winning. Does that seem awful?'

'No, not really,' Velvet said slowly. 'Except that getting what you want is sometimes a kind of losing.'

'We haven't talked like this before, have we?'

'No. I suppose we haven't. You see, I don't want you to turn out like me. All I want is for you to sometimes care about others as well as yourself. That's all.'

'People like Alan, you mean.'

'Well, yes, Alan's one of them. He's the immediate one, but there'll be others, more than you think.'

'But I'm not interested in all that.'

'No, one never is until it happens.'

Although Sarah took her words to heart she still couldn't bring herself to return Alan's increasingly obvious and slavish devotion. Even the fact that he had taken riding lessons in a misguided attempt to please, irritated her – for just as, when we love to an extreme we find it impossible to believe that we ourselves are not loved in return, so when we are loved without loving every fresh evidence of that love only serves to dismay us further.

'You're so funny,' she said to him one afternoon. They had been out riding together and his lack of expertise had spoilt her own enjoyment. 'You're so funny. Taking riding lessons, talking about helping me. That isn't what you really want, is it?'

'Isn't it?' the boy said.

They were sheltering from the rain in one of the empty horse-boxes.

'No,' Sarah said. 'Why don't you just kiss me and get it over with.'

The boy regarded her for a few seconds, then leant forward and kissed her tentatively. Sarah did not respond.

'I'm a disappointment to you, aren't I?' she said.

'No. Not to me.'

'I'm never going to be what people expect me to be. I know exactly what I'm going to do. I've got it all planned. I'm going to get chosen for the British Olympic team.'

'So? You don't have to become a nun as well. Anyway, you can't.'

'Can't what?'

'Ride in the British team. You're American.'

'Wrong. I was born here. I've still got a British passport.'

'Well, all right,' Alan persisted. 'But how d'you know they'll pick you?'

'They will. I'll make sure of that. Hey! it's stopped raining.' She slipped his jacket from her shoulders and handed it back to him. 'Thanks for lending me that. And don't feel badly . . . There's nobody else. Just me.'

She ran towards the house, narrowly missing being run over by the post van.

'Anything for me?' she shouted.

'Anything for me?' John echoed as she entered the hallway. 'Yes, there's something for you. You were obviously expecting something.'

He held out an envelope. The address was typewritten.

'You open it.'

'I never open other people's mail, especially women's.'

'Please!'

She walked away from him and sat on the bottom stair, closing her eyes as though praying.

'D'you know who it's from?'

'I'm guessing . . . Hoping. If it's no, just say it quickly, will you, please?'

John slit the envelope. ' "Dear Miss Brown",' he read aloud, ' "I am writing on behalf of the Combined Training Selection Committee to enquire if you and your horse, Arizona Pie, are available to train as possibles for the British team that will compete at the Ledyard Three-Day Event in America this autumn. If you are able to accept this invitation I would ask that you and your horse arrive at the Windsor Training Establishment on the twentieth of this month for further evalution. Yours sincerely, J. R. Johnson".'

He looked up from the letter. 'You can open your eyes now. What's all this in aid of? What, may I ask, is Ledyard?'

'It's just about the most important Three-Day Event this side of the Olympics, that's all.'

'Oh, well, pardon my ignorance. And they want you to audition for them, do they? Like a chorus line.'

'Nothing like a chorus line.'

'Thank God I'm just an author. At least when I get rejected it's sight unseen. So, since you seem excited beyond all normal expectations, I take it that this letter is good news?'

'It's just the greatest thing that's ever happened,' she said. She snatched the letter from him and raced up to her room.

To want something desperately, to be tested, to feel that

life will be impossible if the object of one's desires is not achieved, is always dangerous for the soul. Some people attempt to climb Everest because, as they say, it is there; others want nothing but wealth and care little how or where they collect it; others still with less avaricious tastes – perhaps desiring nothing more than freedom from fear – are blinded by the same personal sun that shines on all human ambition. At some time or another it burns most of us.

Sarah wanted nothing more than to fulfil her chosen destiny. She was young and impatient and her self-confidence unblunted. She went on the appointed day to the Training Establishment in Windsor Great Park where the British Equestrian Team has traditionally found a home, cantering Arizona across turf and past trees that centuries before had set the Tudors on the path to London. She knew little of English history, but she felt the sense of occasion, for to be a rider, to sit astride a magnificent horse in the peak of condition is, in this mechanical age, to become part of history, part of pageantry, to feel somehow isolated from the rest of scurrying mankind.

She put Arizona through his paces in front of the selection committee and he went beautifully, tuned to her needs, proud of his own strength, glossy with health, responding to Sarah's every touch. She felt her confidence grow and resisted the urge to look at her judges, remembering everything Velvet had told her, riding with a sure instinct. The trial lasted perhaps twenty minutes and then Captain Johnson conferred with his colleagues before they left the field.

'All right, young lady,' he said. 'You can come in now.' She noticed he seldom looked directly at her when he spoke. He was of indeterminate age, somewhat bland, and walked in a way that betrayed his Army background. Had she been more of a native she would have detected traces of a Welsh accent.

She brought Arizona back to him and waited for the verdict.

'Tell me,' Johnson said, 'what made you think you were good enough for us?' He looked at her for the first time, humour crinkling his eyes, but because she was against the sun she could not see his expression.

'What gave you that idea?'

'I've won prizes,' she said in a small voice.

'Have you? What for?'

'Riding.'

'Well, we wouldn't exactly call it riding, would we? Staying on a horse, perhaps. And where did you learn what you call riding?'

'Arizona.'

'Oh, in the colonies. Well, that explains it. Course, you realize they don't admit cowboys to the Olympics . . . I will say one thing, though . . .' He walked round Arizona examining the horse with a practised eye. 'You've some-how managed to get yourself a promising horse.'

He was in front of her once again, but now she could not trust herself to look at him.

'But it's *your* promise we're talking about, isn't it? We have to go back to the beginning, start from scratch. You're not going to cry, are you?'

She shook her head.

'Good. Two things I can't stand in life. Bad losers and criers. Now, when I take somebody – if I take somebody – they come on my terms and work my way. My way happens to be quite frightening to most people. Had you heard that?'

Again she shook her head.

'Well, you're hearing it now. No nonsense, no temperament, no alibis and definitely no question of my admitting that I'm ever wrong! Just hard work, few compliments, lots of shouting, occasional bad language for which I never apologize, and total dedication. Not weeks, not months, but years of total dedication. Like the ballet.'

He hadn't paused once during this monologue, but now he stopped abruptly and his next question caught her off guard.

'Are your parents rich?' he said.

'My parents are dead.'

'Oh. Sorry about that. Who looks after you then?'

'My aunt.'

'Is she well-heeled?'

'I don't know.'

'Better find out, hadn't you? This isn't a cheap sport, you know. And you get precious little help from the general public. They like us to win medals for them, but they don't like to pay . . . So, you'd better go home and have a chat with your aunt, then ring me and tell me when you can start.'

For a second or two she didn't dare answer him, convinced that she had misheard him, that the strain of the morning's events had damaged her hearing.

'When – I can start?' she finally managed to articulate.

'Yes. Isn't that what I said?'

'Does that mean you're going to take me?'

'Well, I'm not going to take your aunt,' Johnson said in a tone that, for him, suggested he might have a well-hidden sense of humour. 'One of you is enough. I daresay we'll make something of you in due course. You're not too bad for a cowboy.'

And with that he walked away.

Sarah leant forward and flung her arms round Arizona's neck. 'D'you hear that? Did you hear what he said? He's going to take us!' She urged him round and they jumped the entire practice course again for the sheer joy of it.

'Look, darling, obviously we'll do everything we can to make it work for you, but it's no use pretending it's going to be easy.'

Sarah nodded. 'No. I do know that, really I do.'

They were all three sitting in John's study having celebrated Sarah's news over dinner. Now it was the time for sober reckoning. Johnson's blunt words about the cost of embarking on such a career were justified and had to be faced. Since The Pie had been retired from stud Velvet had very little independent income and the whole burden fell on John. Novelists, even good novelists – which he was – are lucky if they average the same as a truck driver.

'Getting the money *is* going to be a problem,' Velvet said. 'But it's our problem, not yours, and until we find out exactly what is involved there's no point in getting depressed.'

'I'm not. I mean, it's something just to be chosen by him, isn't it?'

' 'Course it is. Even to be *considered* for the British Team is a tremendous honour. So, you go to bed and let us talk it over.'

'I'm sorry,' Sarah said to John as she kissed him goodnight.

'What're you sorry about?'

'Giving you all this extra worry.'

'I'm not worried. I'm just bankrupt. Only kidding. Go to bed and sleep well.'

Velvet and John stared at each other as the door closed behind Sarah.

'Well . . .' Velvet said.

'Yes. As we were saying when the gas was cut off. What're we talking about, d'you think?'

'Probably a few thousand by the time we're through.'

'Oh, that's nothing. I thought you were going to say a few thousand. Don't feel like winning the Grand National again, do you? Oh, why are things always so complicated? It'd break her heart, wouldn't it, if we didn't find the money?'

'I think it would.'

'Haven't got any more jewellery you can flog, have you?'

'Not even a wedding ring,' Velvet said without malice.

'Ah, well, then I'll just have to think of something brilliant, won't I?'

'You know,' Velvet said, 'when you're not being a disagreeable sod, you're really half way to being very nice.'

'Isn't that funny? Women have always said that. You go to bed, otherwise flattery will get you everywhere. I want to think.'

'Don't stay up too late.'

Left alone, John went and sat at his desk, lit the inevitable cigarette and stared at a pile of manuscript. Work in progress, he thought. But not the sort of work that will produce the cash we need. I never have any luck at roulette, so it's no good trying that old and tested method of getting rich quick. You have to come up with something sensational, Seaton, if you'll pardon the alliteration. Pardoned. But does alliteration sell? What does sell these days?

He switched on his electric typewriter: the familiar hum of the machine always gave him a strange sort of comfort. More from habit than from conviction he put a clean sheet of paper in the rollers and typed the words CHAPTER ONE. There, you see, you're over the first major hurdle, you've made a beginning. Very few writers can get that far so quickly. Now all you need is the odd two hundred thousand words to go with it. They buy in bulk these days, so give them value for money. Give the public what they want, and what they want is . . .

And then it came to him.

EIGHT

The ends sometimes justify the means.

After the event, Velvet was amazed at John's duplicity. For a month following Johnson's acceptance of Sarah he worked solidly, seldom coming to bed before the early hours. There was nothing unusual in this since it followed his normal pattern when starting a new book. He seemed to be in good spirits and answered her enquiries as to progress with what was, for him, surprising good humour. 'What sort of book is it?' Velvet asked.

'Oh, different.'

'A novel?'

'Yes.'

'I thought you'd had novels.'

'Well, I had a good idea and thought I'd follow it through.'

He went to London to have lunch with his publisher, returning later than usual bearing flowers and a bottle of perfume for Velvet and a new hunting crop for Sarah.

'Obviously a successful trip,' they both said.

'You could say that.'

He went back to work with renewed energy, wandering in for meals with a Mona Lisa smile. 'We have to give Sarah an answer,' Velvet reminded him when they were alone together.

'Yes.'

'Well, don't just say yes. I mean, we do. She's been very good about it, she hasn't been pestering us, but I know that she thinks about nothing else.'

'When is she due to report?'

'Next week.'

'She'd better start packing then.'

'What does that mean?'

'Yes, okay, she can go. I've found a way.'

'Well, why didn't you tell us, tell her?'

'I've been busy.'

'You really are the end. Do you mean it? Can I tell her?'

'Yes, tell her.'

'But how, what happened?'

'I caught dear old Roger in a good mood and he gave me a rather generous advance. Like three times more generous than ever before. I think he's getting senile.'

'Darling.' Velvet said. 'That's marvellous. Why on earth didn't you tell me? Obviously he likes the new book?'

'Yes, he thinks this one might sell. I mean, he's not that senile. You know old Roger.'

'How terrific! I can't wait to read it.'

'Well, you'll have to wait a bit longer. I don't want you to read this one until it's finished. It might spoil the flow.'

'So everything's settled then? You are the most extraordinary character. I shall never understand you.'

Sarah echoed the same sentiments the day Velvet drove her and Arizona to the British Training Establishment. 'Isn't Uncle John incredible! Making it all possible like this, from nowhere. Has he always surprised you?'

'Oh, always.'

The real surprise was still to come, however. Preparing for bed one night Velvet glanced at a pile of manuscript on John's bedside table. The title page caught her eye: *Lust Valley* by Jack Delavie.

'What's this?'

John came to the bathroom door.

'What's what? Oh, that. Just something.'

He returned to the basin to finish cleaning his teeth. Velvet read the first few pages.

'Did you write this?'

'No, you can see I didn't. It was written by a character called Jack Delavie.'

'Well, why have you got it?'

'Just doing him a favour.'

'Do I know him?'

'Intimately.'

Velvet frowned. 'Jack Delavie . . . I don't know any Jack Dela . . .' She looked up to find John leaning against the bedpost. 'It's you! Is it you? It isn't, is it?'

'D'you like his style?'

'Well, he writes a mean seduction scene.'

'Does it turn you on?'

'I don't know, I've only read a few pages.'

'Read a few more, spoil yourself. You see, Monsieur Delavie doesn't have my artistic scruples. He's just in it for the money.'

'Where did he do all his research,' Velvet said. 'That's what I'd like to know.'

'Oh, he's been around. Publishers like his stuff, being men of taste and perception. They pay well.'

'They wouldn't pay enough to keep a horse in oats, would they?'

'They might.'

'Oh, you're so devious, Seaton.'

'Just call me Jacques,' John said, affecting an exaggerated French accent.

Whatever preconceived notions Sarah might have had about Captain Johnson's establishment were immediately shattered. In the first place she had fondly imagined that she would be able to lose herself in a crowd for the first few days and be able to make her own mistakes without calling too much attention to herself. She found there were only eight in the class, three other girls and four men. Beth, the senior of the girls, seemed an automatic choice from the start; she had an international reputation and a great horse that had twice carried her to victory at Badminton. Roger, the team captain from the last Olympics, was the oldest of the men; he said little and kept himself to himself. The other two girls, Sue and Marsha, were friendly enough, but behind the welcoming smiles and genuine advice there was no mistaking the rivalry – all the riders were good, they knew they were good, and they intended to prove it to Johnson. Not that Johnson bestowed any favours: all eight were treated equally, that is to say they all suffered.

'Master the basics first!' was his favourite expression, and he took them all back to nursery school. The routine was relentless, with little time left over for any social life.

'Combined training isn't yet a spectator sport, ladies and gentlemen. We don't please the mob like the show jumpers, but, then, they're the gipsies. Flamboyant, death or glory under the arc lights, bands playing, sawdust instead of mud, nice simple fences to knock over . . . Whereas we give them the classical ballet to begin with, which they mistake for weakness; we then take them out into the open air for a taste of the gladiator sports before returning to their beloved arena to illustrate what show jumping is all about. To be a three-day-eventer you have to be touched with madness. You have to love your horse more than you love yourself, you have to match his courage with your own, and you have to believe that what you are attempting is the highest pinnacle of equestrian art. That is why, when you come here and place yourselves in my gifted hands, I take the view that you are all insane enough to suffer the indignities I shall undoubtedly throw at you with a smile, that you will never question my opinion that you are all third-rate but capable of improvement and that when you leave here you will never be the same again. The quality of my mercy is never strained, because I have none. I am not interested in personalities, temperaments or the colour of your eyes. I am only interested in perfection.'

None of the eight, not even Roger, escaped his scorn, for he had no favourites. If they pleased him his silence denoted praise.

'Dressage is not a barn dance, Mr Purcell,' he shouted during one of their regular morning classes in the indoor school. 'You're like a pregnant Tom Mix, and don't ask me who Tom Mix was because I'm too old to tell you. Right! Once more, and not with feeling, spare me that. We don't want emotion, we want beauty of form.'

After the practical lessons he returned to the blackboard and patiently explained the theory.

'Some of you have come here with the impression that Dressage is boring compared with the greater glories of the cross-country event. That's because you lack sophistication, amongst other things. The origins of Dressage are deeply rooted in the classical tradition and you have to think of any Dressage test as if it were a concerto by Bach . . . That's Bach the composer, Mr Armstrong, not bark as in dog! To perform it well you have to have an appreciation of the marriage of man and animal. It's an emotional experience, but emotion under control. I hope you're suitably impressed by the quality of my language, I'm not just a pretty face, you know.'

He swung round and stared at Sarah. 'The cross-country, on the other hand, is thought by some . . . Miss Brown . . . to be an opportunity to display carefree abandon. This is a mistake for which I would cheerfully reintroduce capital punishment. It is a test of brains and since horses are only marginally less stupid than some of the people who ride them – an observation that carries with it the experience of a lifetime – I would urge you not to sit on your brains, but to use them . . .'

In her letters home to Velvet and John Sarah revealed little of her real feelings, and never mentioned her loneliness, her sense of being isolated from the rest of the group, for like most people who lack friends she had not yet grasped the vital lesson that the fault lay within herself. Her will to succeed, which approached an obsession, blinded her to all else and yet there were moments when she envied the ease with which Beth and Susan could divorce themselves from Johnson's strictures the moment classes were over. She wrote nothing of this to Velvet, however. '*Everything is terrific here,*' she wrote. '*We seem to work twenty-five hours a day and there isn't time for anything else. Competition is fierce because everybody wants to impress the great Captain Johnson, who is one of those very British British – everybody says he's got a velvet fist in an iron glove. My social life is something to behold – there's a four-letter word for it which I'm sure you can guess, since we spend long hours mucking out in the stables after class has finished. Arizona is fine and the envy of all. He's definitely in a class by himself and is getting very conceited. Don't think I'm not having fun, and don't think I'm not still grateful for making it all possible . . .*'

As training progressed they spent more and more time in Windsor Great Park, moving from single jumps to simulated cross-country courses. Sarah enjoyed the early mornings best, when they exercised the horses, riding through misted avenues of trees. It was then she felt that she and Arizona were the only two inhabiting the earth. He moved so effortlessly, anticipating her commands, responding as though by telepathy. Sometimes when the sun burnt through the ground mist they would gallop into a clearing and she would suddenly be presented with a view of Windsor Castle in the distance. At other times they exercised in the steep sand pits close to the lake at Virginia Water, and always there was the excitement of daring the impossible, pushing herself and Arizona to the limit, returning to the stables exhausted, a little frightened sometimes, but always exhilarated. Johnson missed nothing of importance, never relaxed, rigidly imposed his standards. 'Sometimes,' Roger said, 'I don't feel I'm jumping fences, I'm jumping him, and the trouble with him is, he knows it. That's what he wants us to feel. You see, he was the best there was, in his day. And you can't fool him. I've tried and it never works.'

But even Johnson was capable of surprising them by suddenly showing them another side of his character. After a particularly gruelling session in the sand-pits when they had been closely observed by other members of the Selection Committee, Johnson called them together for what they imagined was to be a sarcastic post-mortem.

'There's hope,' he said. 'You weren't brilliant this morning, but on the other hand you weren't entirely appalling. And just to prove to you what a basically soft-hearted character I am, I'm cancelling class tomorrow. Make the most of it, because as you know the milk of human kindness has to be forced into my veins under pressure. So off you go . . . Except, I just want a word with you, young lady.'

He crooked a finger in Sarah's direction, then waited until the others had dispersed.

'Don't look so scared, otherwise I'll have to change my whole personality. Now, whatever else you may think of me, I'll never tell you anything but the truth. So, let's start with the good news. You've worked very hard and you've made extraordinary progress.'

'Thank you.'

'Don't thank me. It's your bottom that's sore, not mine. Before you're through you'll ride well enough to make anybody's team . . . but the thing that worries me about you has nothing to do with riding. D'you know what I'm talking about?'

Sarah shook her head.

'It has to do with your personality. You're too preoccupied with yourself. Nobody can play this game on a hooray-for-me-to-hell-with-you basis. You need the team, they need you. It's like the war. The loners seldom made it, most of them got killed quicker than the rest. Think about it.'

He walked from her.

She thought about what he had said on the journey back to Mothecombe, weighing the compliment against the criticism. If she wanted to believe the one then she had to believe the other. She did want to believe that her riding had improved, therefore she had to believe Johnson's opinion of her as a person.

John was the only one in the house when she arrived and he shouted 'Darling?' from his study as she entered.

'It's not darling,' Sarah said. 'It's me.'

'Well, no complaints. What's happened, why are you back?'

'We got given the day off. Captain Johnson suddenly went ape and cancelled class.'

'His loss is our gain. How's it going?'

'Okay, I guess. Next week is the big crunch.'

'Next week?'

'Yeah. They make the selection next week. Is there anything to eat? I'm starving.'

'Don't they feed you down there?'

'The horses eat better.'

She wandered through into the kitchen and John, welcoming the interruption, left his desk and followed her.

'You depressed about something?' he asked. 'You sound a bit down.'

'No, not really.'

He opened the fridge door and looked inside. 'Well, now, we have the gourmet peanut butter. Something which looks like a very nasty piece of cheese . . . and in fact *is* a very nasty piece of cheese . . .'

'I'll make a sandwich, that's fine.'

'You want what you call the jelly and we call the jam? I'll never understand that.'

'Why don't you try it, it's a taste sensation.'

'All right, why not? Cut me one of those wedges. So, you're not depressed?'

'Yes and no . . . Can I ask you something?'

'Don't give me as much as that, I'm a beginner. Sorry, yes, what's bothering you?'

'Well,' Sarah handed him a large slice of bread spread liberally with peanut butter and jelly. 'I don't understand what makes me tick. See, I know what I'm doing wrong, but I can't seem to do any thing about it.'

'What d'you think you're doing wrong?'

'I don't make friends. At first I never wanted friends. Arizona was enough, I didn't want anything else . . . and now that I do, I don't know how you go about it.' She looked up at him. He was wiping jelly from his chin.

'Did you ever have that problem?'

'Are we going by sex? I mean, for "friends" do we read "boy friends"? Because I never had any boy friends.'

'Any. Either. I mean, I wouldn't be picky.'

'Well, now . . . You know, this isn't bad, I could be converted.' He finished his messy sandwich and licked his fingers. 'You can't – how shall I put it? – You can't wake up one morning and say "Today, I'm going to make a couple of friends". It doesn't happen like that. It's like falling in love, in a way, it sometimes takes you by surprise and sometimes it's there all the time and you just haven't seen it. Look, to tell you the truth, I don't know, you can't know for anybody else. All I can tell you is that it will happen . . . You just have to find somebody who likes your brand of peanut butter.'

'You want another?'

'Why not? Let's go on a jag.'

Sarah started to cut him another lumpy slice of bread. 'See, another thing,' she said, 'I don't have any nerves, not when I'm riding. That's the only time it's all going for me, when I don't have any doubts at all . . . D'you think I'll lose that, like Velvet?'

John hesitated before answering. 'Did she tell you she'd lost her nerve?' Sarah nodded. 'Well, that was a kind of white lie. She didn't really lose her nerve, she lost a child.'

Sarah stared at him.

'Not my child,' John continued hurriedly. 'While she was married. She fell, you see. She was riding, riding The Pie, and she shouldn't have been. After that she couldn't have children, and then I came along and I didn't help all that much, because my little hang-up is I'm frightened of anything signed and sealed and permanent . . . Listen, this peanut butter's like a truth drug!'

They were both silent for a while, and then John said, 'To write and to live . . . are very different, you know.'

'I've given myself a choice,' Mike said. 'If Johnson doesn't pick me, I'll either go to Japan and get massaged to death, or else I'll become a Liberal MP. Two foolproof methods of suicide.'

They were all assembled in the indoor ring to hear Johnson's verdict. The day of reckoning had finally arrived.

'I just wish it was over,' Beth said. 'One way or the other.'

'Oh, you're all right. He'll choose you.'

'Why do you say that?'

'He goes for the older women,' Mike said.

Sarah smiled uneasily. She was too tense to join in the general banter. Looking round at the other seven faces she noticed that even Roger seemed uncharacteristically nervous.

Johnson suddenly appeared in the doorway and all conversation ceased. He started talking immediately. 'I'll make this as quick and as painless as possible. Despite all the evidence to the contrary, I don't enjoy these occasions. They remind me of the time when I left my first wife – it was a choice between her and the horses and the horses cost less to feed . . . and don't think you have to laugh, my rare jokes always have tragic undertones . . .'

He turned and faced them all. 'So . . . the team for Ledyard. It was a difficult decision because naturally under my tutelage you're all brilliant. I was choosing a team, and the components had to fit. The final selection is as follows: Beth . . . Howard . . . Mike . . . and Roger.'

He paused and looked round the eight faces yet again, passing Sarah and then coming back to her. 'The reserve rider will be Sarah.'

Sarah's feelings were understandably mixed. It was less than she had hoped for, but more than she had feared. I wasn't rejected, she thought. And 'reserve rider' means what it says. Reserves get used. She remembered football matches her father had taken her to in Arizona, when the reserves were always called upon.

'Congratulations to you five,' Johnson continued, 'and commiserations to those who didn't make it this time. Don't take it too badly, because the great thing about this sport is it's here to stay. And thank you all.'

Perhaps his voice quavered a little on the last sentence, as though he had betrayed himself by such a slight show of emotion. He strode from the ring without looking back.

They left from Stanstead Airport five days before the Ledyard Event was due to start. Everybody was on hand to supervise the horses being loaded into the cargo jet and Sarah was amazed by the efficiency of it all and the way in which Arizona behaved. Although he had never seen an aircraft before let alone flown in one, he allowed himself to be led into the special horse-box without any show of temperament, in stark contrast to Roger's horse Gold Dust who required a great deal of patient persuasion. The boxes were fork-lifted to the height of the cargo door and then rolled into position inside the open cabin. In addition to the five riders the official party included several grooms, Johnson and the team vet, Tim. Everything was checked and double checked, since Event horses are extremely valuable and international regulations concerning their transport by air are very strict.

Once in position the horse-boxes occupied most of the cargo area, the passengers being seated to the rear of the aircraft and attended to by a single stewardess.

The grooms occupied the special compartments in the horse-boxes in order to reassure their charges. The horses themselves wore protective headgear.

Once the seat belt sign had been switched off Johnson

went forward to the cockpit area to speak to the Captain of the aircraft, a veteran of the wartime RAF, as were many of the commercial pilots who no longer flew scheduled passenger routes.

'Everything okay back there?' the Captain asked.

'Fine.' Like others before him Johnson was impressed by the casual attitude of the aircrew which in this case consisted of a co-pilot and navigator, both much younger men than the Captain.

'We going to have a smooth trip?' Johnson asked.

'Should do. Could be some clear air turbulence. Just a bit. The weather report's too good. We're always suspicious when the old Met man gives us a clean sheet, aren't we, George?'

'Too true,' the co-pilot said.

The plane was on automatic by now and the Captain swivelled round in his seat. 'I know what I wanted to ask you,' he said. 'Your lot worth having a bet on?'

'Bet?' Johnson expostulated. 'They're not race horses, they're Eventers. Don't you know the difference?'

'No. Golf is my game. My only contact with the gee-gees is I fly them, sometimes have a flutter, and on occasions, I believe, I've eaten them. During the war, that is.'

'Barbarian,' Johnson said.

'No. Quite tasty, as I recall. Bit on the sweet side.'

Back in the passenger cabin, the vet had left his seat to check that all the horses were contented. Arizona seemed totally unconcerned in his alien surroundings and was eating quite happily, as were three of the others. Only Roger's Gold Dust seemed unduly restless and fretful. The vet had given him a mild tranquillizer before take-off, but it seemed to have had little or no effect. As he explained to Sarah, although permitted within certain limits, the use of any sort of drugs where horses are concerned has to be very carefully judged.

'He'll settle down,' Roger said. 'He's such a prima donna, he always plays up when I take him abroad. Now, just behave yourself, d'you hear,' he said as he stroked the horse's neck with a soothing rhythm. 'You've got a first class ticket and they've served your meal before mine.'

He took his own seat again as the stewardess came round with coffee, but no sooner had he and the rest of the team got their trays than the plane gave a sudden lurch.

'Doesn't it always happen!' Mike said. 'Like clockwork. It must be me. I've never been on a flight when I didn't get a meal in my lap. The day I get off a plane with a clean suit will be a miracle.'

Up in the cockpit Johnson peered through the small windscreen at the apparently calm sky ahead.

'Is that the clear-air stuff you mentioned?'

'Yes,' the Captain said. 'Doesn't show on the radar.' He made a slight adjustment to some controls.

'What did you do then?'

'Then? I just changed the heat in the cabin.'

It was all a mystery to Johnson. He felt out of his depth. I'm only really happy, he thought, when I've got a stable floor under my feet. These ex-RAF types are so deliberately casual. All an act, of course.

'Had a strange cargo last week,' the Captain said conversationally as the plane gave another lurch. 'We had a full load of assorted frozen sandwiches. Picked them up in Manchester.'

The plane lurched again, but the other two members of the crew paid no attention, seeming to be more interested in the rest of the Captain's story.

'Took them to the Gulf, didn't we, George? Part of the arms race, I suppose. The new British secret weapon. Can you imagine anybody wanting to import frozen British sandwiches?'

Johnson attempted a polite smile, but his mind was elsewhere. The next, unexpected lurch, when it came pushed him back against the cabin door. He heard crockery going down with a smash somewhere.

'Look,' the Captain said. 'Probably better if you go and strap yourself in for a bit until we get through this stuff. Shouldn't last long. I'll try and get clearance to climb above it. Trouble is, you sometimes climb into it. Like getting remarried, as George knows to his cost.'

They were still laughing amongst themselves at this latest example of the Captain's wit as Johnson pulled open the cockpit door and stumbled to the rear of the fuselage. There was very little room between the horse-boxes and the side of the cargo cabin and several times en route he was thrown with some force and nearly lost his balance. Some of the grooms were looking a little anxious.

'Soon be through it,' Johnson said with false confidence. 'Just make sure the horses are all right.'

Roger hadn't returned to his place when the Seat Belt sign went on again, but instead had stayed by Gold Dust who was reacting very badly to the turbulence. As Johnson came alongside the box, which was the last one to the rear of the aircraft and closest to the passenger seats, Roger confessed his growing anxiety.

'I've never known him like this,' he said. 'Steady, boy, steady. Now just be steady, there!'

'I'll get Tim,' Johnson said, but the vet had anticipated him.

'Look, I don't want to give him another shot so soon after the first,' he said.

'No, I realize that,' Johnson said. 'I mean, it's your decision entirely, but keep a close eye on him, will you.'

Beth had moved to the seat next to Sarah.

'What happens if any of the horses get really frightened?' Sarah asked.

'Oh, Tim'll take care of them,' Beth said, concealing her own mounting anxiety. 'He's marvellous.'

Before the words were out of her mouth the plane seemed to drop straight down for several seconds. Hand baggage and tea trays went sliding all over the place and instinctively Sarah gripped Beth's arm.

'It's all right,' Beth said. 'I've been in this sort of thing before. These planes ride out anything.'

Then it was her turn to show alarm as Gold Dust kicked violently against the rear panel of his box. The noise seemed to be amplified in the confined space. They heard one of the grooms shout from up front and Howard and Mike slipped their seat belts and slithered forward to investigate. The regular hum of the jet's engines changed pitch as the Captain gave them extra throttle; to Sarah the combination began to assume the proportions of a nightmare. She could see Roger, Tim and Johnson struggling with Gold Dust, who was rearing in his box-stall. His protective headgear – a thick layer of foam rubber – had worked loose and, as he reared, his head thudded against the plastic ceiling of the fuselage. Again he kicked back and Sarah saw the metal retaining bolts holding the locking bars in position suddenly jump out. She screamed and Beth put a hand over her eyes and cradled her.

Tim struggled back to his seat to retrieve his case of instruments.

'You'll have to give him another shot,' Johnson shouted.

'I know, but it's dicey,' Tim answered. 'You know that. If I give him the shot he needs there's always the chance I'll kill him. On the other hand, if it's not big enough he'll kick the plane to pieces.'

'There must be something in between, isn't there?' Roger said. He needed all his strength to hold on to Gold Dust now.

'Not in the book there isn't. But, here goes, I'll try and judge it.'

'Let me go and have another word with the Captain,' Johnson said. He went forward. Tim filled a hypodermic.

'Try and hold him steady,' he told Roger.

He got the needle into the horse but before he could empty the syringe Gold Dust reared violently, knocking him off balance and the hypodermic went flying. The aircraft was still battling against the turbulence and now Gold Dust started to go mad, lashing his hind legs against the rear of the box. Frenzy increased his strength and the retaining bolts gave way. The metal locking bar flew across the passenger compartment, narrowly missing the terrified stewardess. There was nothing anybody could do with the horse after that – the best that Roger and Tim could manage was to hang on to his headstall for dear life, but it was an unequal struggle.

Johnson returned with the Captain. Both were appalled by what they found, for by now Gold Dust had completely shattered the rear of the box and although Roger and Tim still had hold of him it was patently obvious that they were losing the battle. As with the Captain of a ship, the Captain of an aircraft has the ultimate decision in any emergency. A mad horse in a pressurized jet at thirty thousand feet is more dangerous than a hijacker, and as Johnson rushed to give what help he could to the other two men he knew what the answer had to be.

'Look,' the Captain shouted above the noise. 'I'm sorry to lay this on you, but you're going to have to destroy that horse. And if it helps, I'll make that an order. Do it and do it quickly before the rest of them go berserk. We've got a long way to go. I'm sorry, but there it is.'

He left them to go back to his controls. While Johnson and Roger struggled together, Tim reached down into his case for the humane killer.

'What're they going to do?' Sarah said. 'What're they going to do?'

'Don't watch,' Beth said. She put her arms round the younger girl. 'It's soon over, and it doesn't hurt, they don't feel anything, I promise you. It's all done so quickly.'

Roger held on as tightly as he could as Tim raised the humane pistol, talking all the time, talking for the last time, to the horse he loved. Only at the final moment did he turn his head away. There was very little sound and then Gold Dust was suddenly silent, the halter rope went limp, sliding through Roger's raw palms. He felt nothing. It was as if the whole world had gone silent and he slumped against the side of the cabin and tears poured down his face, the sort of tears grown men give way to when grief is absolute.

It was a sombre arrival at Boston airport. Word of the tragedy had been radioed ahead and there was a sympathetic gathering of other riders from opposing teams to greet them. As the British team got into the waiting cars two members of the American team came up to express their sympathy.

'Whose horse was it?' one of them asked.

'Roger Peacock's,' Beth said.

'You mean Gold Dust? Gee, that's terrible. That's always been my nightmare. Will you tell him how sorry I am, I don't want to bother him myself, not right now.'

He stared past Beth to Sarah, then stood back as Johnson gave the signal for the cars to move off.

The Ledyard International Horse Trials are unique,

attracting as they do the finest Event horses and riders from most sporting nations. They are held on a private farm in South Hamilton, Massachusetts and although they have only been held a few times, have quickly established themselves as a major showcase. The setting at Ledyard is totally different from its nearest rivals and since the trials are traditionally held during the splendour of a New England autumn the many thousands of spectators who flock to South Hamilton are treated not only to a feast of great riding, but also to a spectacle of natural beauty that is unsurpassed. The organizers take infinite pains to construct a cross-country course that is not only an exacting series of tests for horse and rider, but also possesses pictorial beauty in its own right. The fences are complicated in their design and made from a variety of different timber, here one built from silver birch, here another in the shape of an oak picture-frame in the midst of multi-coloured maples, yet another in the form of a harvest wagon garlanded with sheaves of wheat. Ledyard is informal, graceful, giving as it does a glimpse of a bygone age, for on the third and last day the show-jumping is preceded by a display of coaching horses and their antique vehicles, brass bands, cheer-leaders, formation dancers. Craft stalls dot the perimeter of the show-jumping field and the atmosphere is more akin to a country fair than an international sporting event. The alchemy works, for Ledyard imparts some of its natural magic to the competitors and few go away disappointed.

Since New Englanders are justly famous for their hospitality, a welcoming dinner party had been arranged for the visiting teams, but it was an invitation that Johnson felt he could not accept in the circumstances.

Once the remaining British horses had been stabled for the night he called his team together. 'I explained we might not feel up to it,' he said. 'And of course they understand. I don't want to take any hasty decisions, but obviously first thing in the morning, when we've all had a good night's rest, we have to sort things out. You girls okay?'

Beth and Sarah both nodded.

'Good. Well, I'll say goodnight then. Take care of yourselves.'

'Do you think I'll get to ride?' Sarah asked when she and Beth were alone in their room.

'No idea. I expect we'll know soon enough.'

'That boy who talked to you at the airport . . .'

'Scott Saunders, you mean?'

'Is that Scott Saunders? He's the American team captain.'

'Yes.'

'He's good, isn't he?'

'He's very good,' Beth said.

'Have you ever ridden against him?'

'Not only ridden against him, but on one particularly happy occasion, ridden over him.'

'What does that mean.'

'Nothing much. You'll find out.'

'No, tell me. I hate riddles.'

'Goodnight,' Beth said, refusing to be drawn. She switched out her light. Sarah got into her own bed. She had never felt less like sleep. From far away she could hear the sound of a dance band. The altered circumstances of her life suddenly became unbearably romantic and she was consumed with the feeling that her life was about to change. The fact of being back in the country she had once counted as her own produced a sense of mystery. Listening to the music drifting across the damp lawns she found herself reminded of Fitzgerald's Gatsby, as though destiny in the shape of the unknown Scott Saunders waited outside in the darkness, a figure as enigmatic as the hero of her favourite novel, fiction merging into fact as imagination took hold. Then the images became confused as sleep claimed her. Scott's face became Johnson's and he in turn was replaced by Roger. The horror of the horse's death in the plane overlapped into the remembered death of her parents all those years before. Then Johnson returned to the front of her mind and she tried to imagine what his decision would be in the morning. Her last thought was of Arizona. If anything happened to Arizona, she thought, I'd want to die with him, and sleep, when it came, was troubled, the dream pictures mixed like cards in a pack.

'There's no sense in dwelling on yesterday's tragedy,' Johnson said. His manner was brusque, as of old. 'Roger . . . everybody here knows what you're feeling and of course we feel for you, but unfortunately sorrow doesn't win competitions, otherwise I'd be a three-time gold medallist. We've come a long way and you've all worked too hard to let something like this destroy our chances. It's just that the order of things has changed.'

He turned back to Roger. 'This is what I've decided. You'll ride Magic, but I'll nominate you to go second instead of last.'

Roger nodded. 'That makes sense.'

'Sarah,' Johnson continued, 'I'm entering you as an individual competitor. It'll give you the feel of an international event without the responsibility of worrying about the team . . . Yes, what is it, Mike?'

'You obviously haven't heard.'

'What?'

'Well, Tim thinks there could be some doubt about Magic. I thought he'd told you.'

'No, I've been with the Committee since breakfast. Where is he now?'

'In the stables.'

'Let's go.'

When they arrived at the stables they were greeted by a glum-looking Tim.

'Johnny, I'm sorry, but it's not good news. He's slipped his stifle. You see for yourself, he can hardly bear to put any weight on it.'

Johnson bent and examined the horse. 'Is there any chance at all?'

'In three days? No way.'

'It's just not our trip, is it?'

He walked away from the group, unable to trust his voice for the moment.

'What now, Johnny?' Roger asked.

'We don't have any choice, do we? You'll have to ride Arizona. You've got three days to get used to him. Let's hope the jinx stops here. Get on with it.'

Sarah stepped forward as Johnson was about to leave. 'Could I say something, please?'

'If it's to the point, yes. If it's personal, no.'

'It's just that nobody but me has ever ridden Arizona. I just don't know how he'd go for somebody else.'

Johnson stared through her. 'He's a team horse and Roger is our most experienced rider.'

'So I don't get to ride at all?'

'Exactly. Anything else?'

Sarah shook her head. Johnson turned and left.

Mike put an arm round her shoulders, but she was beyond comfort.

She got up at dawn the following morning to help Roger

prepare Arizona and watched at a distance as he warmed up the horse before jumping him over the practice course. She had to admit that Roger was a superb horseman and that Arizona seemed to accept his authority immediately. In some ways that was a greater betrayal than Johnson's, and she left the scene and went back to her room. Beth and the others were also out with their horses. She felt completely isolated.

A party had been arranged for that evening, just an informal gathering to help relax the competitors, in the social tradition of Ledyard where every effort was made to avoid the stuffier forms of protocol.

'Why don't you change your mind and come?' Beth said. 'It'd take you out of it.'

'I just know I'd be a wet blanket,' Sarah said.

'I'll do your hair for you. Come on.'

'No thanks. Thanks all the same.'

'They've got a really hot band.'

'I can hear it. I know I'm being dreary, so don't take any notice, just go and enjoy it.'

'Okay.'

Sarah sat in her room, but the sounds of the party seemed to intensify her mood, and after a while she wandered in the direction of the stables. Arizona whickered softly at her approach, and she thought how smart he looked in his brand-new rug with the Union Jack emblazoned on it.

She gave him some lumps of sugar and stroked his favourite spot behind his ears.

'Now just because I'm not going to be with you,' she said, 'I don't want any acting up. D'you hear? You just go out there with Roger and show them how brilliant you are. Because one of us has got to. Are you listening?'

'Why aren't you at the party?' a voice behind her said.

She turned quickly. Johnson had come into the stables unobserved.

'No particular reason. I just thought I'd look in on Arizona.'

Johnson nodded. 'I don't suppose you cared overmuch for the decision I made today.'

'You did what you thought best.'

'Best for the team, best for Roger . . . and best for you, too, although I don't expect you to believe that right now . . .'

'No, I don't,' Sarah said honestly.

'Oh, you ride Arizona better than Roger, no doubt about it. You'll always ride him better than anybody else, because he's your horse. Nevertheless Roger's got two things going for him that you haven't. Can you tell me what they are?'

'Experience?'

'Judgement, really. Judgement. Knowing how fast you can push a green horse over a strange course and still finish. But there's something else. Roger has the ability to sacrifice his own vanity – and that's saying a lot – the ability to sacrifice his vanity for the good of the team.'

Sarah took this in, and then some of her resentment surfaced again. 'Well, I still don't get it. How can he help the team more if he gets less out of Arizona than I could?'

'Because Roger will *finish* on this horse of yours. Maybe not brilliantly, but he'll get round and we'll have a team score . . . You might get round faster, but then, on the other hand, you might not get round at all.'

'It still seems pretty unfair.'

'Yes,' Johnson said, 'well, it's a pretty unfair process all round, isn't it – growing up? Everybody thinks they know better than you, don't they? Me included. As you've seen, I think I know better than most people, and that's my problem . . . But, you will ride for me one day, dear Sarah,

I've promised you that. And you'll not only ride for me, you'll ride for the greater glory of the sport and the honour of the team. Those aren't just empty words.'

He paused by Arizona's stall and patted the horse before turning back to her.

'There was a very interesting ... a very wise Frenchman, who had a great deal to do with the modern Olympics. His name was Coubertin, Baron de Coubertin, and he said – I might not be able to quote him correctly – but he said the most important thing in the Games is not the winning, but the taking part ... just as the most important thing in life is not the triumph but the struggle ... That's to say, the essential thing is not to have conquered, but to have fought well. Does that make any sense to you? It makes a great deal of sense to me. You see, I used to be a bit like you, a bit of a grandstander, only nobody took the trouble to tell me, as I'm attempting to tell you, that the sun didn't actually shine out of my backside. I wish they had, it might have saved me a lot of bother ... Well, lecture over.'

He put out a hand. 'Now, then, if you'd like to put on a party frock you can take me to the dance. I won't be the youngest you'll dance with, but I'll certainly be the safest. What d'you say, cowboy?'

Sarah hesitated a second, then took his hand. Together they left the stable.

Having got to the dance, she enjoyed it. As Beth said, it was a good band, and by the time she and Johnson arrived everything was swinging. Johnson wasn't exactly Fred Astaire, but he had a certain flamboyant confidence which disguised his inability to execute anything other than a foxtrot. Then a young man wearing the American team blazer cut in.

'Come on, Johnny, you can't monopolize the talent all night,' the young man said, and Sarah turned to find herself confronted by Scott Saunders. 'Time you were in bed anyway.'

'Make one false move with her,' Johnson said, 'and you'll never ride again. Thank you, Sarah, that was delightful and I'm sorry you've now got to take second best.'

Sarah and Scott waited for the band to strike up again, then joined the crush on the floor.

'Well, that was easier than I expected,' Scott said. 'I'm Scott Saunders, by the way.'

'I know.'

'How d'you know?'

'Beth and I were talking about you.'

'And you're Sarah . . . the British secret weapon.'

'So secret,' Sarah said, 'I'm not even riding. Roger's got my horse.'

'That isn't a British accent.'

'Would you believe Cave Creek, Arizona?'

'You defected, huh?'

'I escaped.'

'You still kept your accent.'

'Oh, I kept everything,' Sarah said. 'I don't give anything away.'

She said it with a smile, but the message was loud and clear.

NINE

The weather wasn't kind to Ledyard that year. For most of the three days it rained solidly, turning the dressage rings and the cross-country course into a dangerous quagmire. To ask a horse to perform elegant dressage movements on turf transformed into a shifting bog is like asking a ballet dancer to do a *pas de deux* on a surf board. Those spectators dedicated and hardy enough to sit it out huddled beneath brightly-coloured umbrellas, but there were times when everybody concerned – riders, judges and audience – could scarcely see the length of the ring. It was a heartbreaking sight and devastatingly sad for the organizers who had put in two years' hard work to prepare the event. But for all that the riders and horses put on a show of ignoring the elements and although their immaculate riding clothes were sodden, they rode with panache and the spectators applauded their courage and fortitude.

Roger and Arizona didn't do well in the Dressage. It wasn't Roger's lack of preparation with the horse, or the foul weather – for after all that was common to all the competitors – but due mostly to the fact that Arizona, highly strung and tuned for the major test of the cross-country, was impatient with the disciplines so vital to good dressage and never really settled. Beth and Howard and

Mike fared better, but by the end of the first day the British team was well down the list.

It rained spasmodically throughout the second day when the roads and tracks and the cross-country course were attempted. The going was rough, for the fences would have been difficult enough in ideal conditions, and it wasn't long before tragedy marred the day. One of the horses fell dead of a heart attack as it took a jump, trapping its rider beneath its twitching carcass. Another rider was taken away in an ambulance, with a broken back. There were many other spills, fortunately not so serious, and a large number of eliminations.

Sarah and Johnson moved around the large course from fence to fence, trying to keep track of the field and their own team in particular. Roger and Arizona completed the course without mishap, but Arizona had two refusals and time faults. Beth, Howard and Mike also got round with Howard the only British rider to finish with no penalty points. By the end of the second day the British team had moved up into fifth place and were still in there with a chance.

On the last day conditions improved and for the first two hours the sun painted the brilliant autumn countryside. The show-jumping field dried out somewhat, but only the display of horse-drawn coaches benefited, for by the time the preliminary events had finished and the last drum-majorette had strutted from the scene, the rain commenced again. Huddled together in protective clothing, Sarah and Johnson and a dwindling band of stalwarts kept their seats to the end. The American team held onto and improved their lead and although Mike and Beth had good rounds, neither went clear and it was obvious that unless both Roger and Howard rode faultlessly any chance of second or third place was out of the question. Roger and Arizona began well, taking the first seven fences in great style, and Sarah's heart leapt with pride. By now she had completely forgotten her own disappointment, and she willed Roger to succeed in her place. Perhaps because of the treacherous going, perhaps because of an unfamiliar rider, Arizona swerved out just before the eighth fence and although Roger, fully in control, brought him back in the tightest of turns, the splendid rhythm had gone. He jumped the eighth at the second attempt, but was out of stride for the next and tipped a bar. After that, disaster followed disaster, and he demolished the triple like a child scattering toy bricks.

Howard, riding last for the British team, retrieved something by a clear round, but at the end of the day they were placed third. The presentation, always a stirring spectacle at Ledyard with the winning teams preceded by mounted standard-bearers, took place in lashing rain on a sodden battlefield.

Because of all the things that had happened since they left England, Sarah came away from Ledyard with a greater respect for the dangers of the sport and enhanced understanding of what Johnson had tried to teach her. Thinking over the entire sequence of events, from the death of Roger's horse on the 'plane to the ultimate disappointment of not riding Arizona at all, she saw the rightness and justice of Johnson's decision, but couldn't stop herself wondering if her participation might have made any difference. To fail was one thing, but not to have the chance to fail was another. 'I guess I'll never know,' she thought.

Before leaving Ledyard she attempted to find Scott again, but he and the other members of the American team had already scattered, for most of them were riding in other events. As she was about to catch the flight back to London she felt something – not homesickness, not nostalgia, or a return of sorrow, but more a feeling of hollowness – when the airport announcer relayed details of the departure of a flight to Phoenix, Arizona. How far away it all seemed, a life that belonged to somebody else.

The life she returned to at Mothecombe unsettled her. She was restless, on edge, and she found that she missed the companionship and the challenge of being with the team. Long rides with Arizona across the flat sands of the estuary only served to intensify a growing need to prove herself. She threw herself single-mindedly into the task of schooling Arizona to the peak of perfection, knowing that their chance of being selected for the Olympic team depended on his performance in the big competitions that lay ahead that season. Johnson had given her a glimpse of his 'greater glories' and she was avid for more.

Velvet and to a lesser extent John noticed the change in her. Some of her old moodiness returned; that rebellious quality, so necessary for anybody in competitive sport as long as it is controlled, bordered on arrogance in her case. She had grown apart from her friends in the village and when she was not exercising Arizona or taking part in trials she withdrew completely.

A chance meeting with Alan Wilson one afternoon when she was riding Arizona along the edge of the sea at low tide (for he loved wading through the gentle surf) drove her further into herself. He was over-anxious to score with his own news.

'I'm getting married,' he said and watched her closely for her reaction. The announcement was a mixture of defiance and the need to wound. Sarah knew that, knew how easily she could twist him back if she so wanted, but the certainty of her instincts meant there was no longer any fun in it.

'Anybody I know?'

'Sheila Gardner. Remember her?'

'Oh, yes. Well, congratulations. How's the riding going?'

'I gave that up,' he said. 'Too expensive and there didn't seem much point.' He realized that her question was not without that malice that comes so easily to young girls, that she had pierced his vulnerability. He gave as good as he got. 'By the way, we were hoping to see you on television.'

'You will one day.'

'What happened at Ledyard?'

'Nothing. Well, nice to see you again.' She spurred Arizona across the sands before he could reply. He watched her go, knowing she was lost to him forever.

The chance encounter had nettled Sarah for all that and she returned to the house in a foul mood. Neither Velvet nor John was about. She wandered about, picked at some leftovers in the kitchen, then went to find a book to read in John's study. Passing his desk she glanced down at a manuscript by the side of his typewriter. The title and the unfamiliarity of the author's name – *Sin is Here to Stay* by Jack Delavie – made her pause and pick it up. She stayed by the desk while she read the first two or three pages, then took the manuscript to her room.

She was still reading it an hour later when Velvet returned and came in search of her. Hearing Velvet approach up the circular staircase, Sarah concealed the manuscript under the cushions on her day bed.

'There you are,' Velvet said. 'I thought you must be in by now. Have a good ride?'

'Okay.'

'What's wrong?'

'Nothing.'

'You worried because you haven't heard anything from Johnson?'

'No.'

'You know what they say – no news is good news. He'll pick you again. You know you're a possibility for the Olympics. Coming home after all that excitement at Ledyard was bound to be an anti-climax. I tell you what, why don't you and I go up to London and see a show? Cheer us both up.'

'I have to train.'

'You don't have to train every minute of the day.'

'I need a new saddle.'

'What's wrong with the old one?'

'It just isn't good enough.'

'Saddles don't win medals.'

'I didn't say they did.'

Velvet stared at her. 'Why're you in such a stinking mood?'

'I'm not.'

'Seems like it to me.' Velvet got up from her chair and started to leave the room.

'Who's Jack Delavie?' Sarah asked.

Velvet paused in the doorway.

'Why do you ask that?'

Sarah produced the manuscript from under the cushion.

'I found this on John's desk. It's him, he's Jack Delavie, isn't he?'

'What if he is?'

'I read some of it and it's real disgusting trash. How can he write such stuff?'

Velvet came back into the room. Her voice was flat with anger. 'Don't you ever say that! Not ever! As a matter of fact John agrees with you, he's not too proud of it either, but he's entitled to think that, and you're not. And I'll tell you why not. That "trash" as you call it, has paid for everything you've done in the past year and will probably pay for the new saddle you think you have to have. So before you pass too many smart moral judgements, just remember the world doesn't owe you a living. Nothing's for free and some people pay more than others . . . So don't ever mention it again!'

She took the manuscript from Sarah's hand and slammed the door when she left.

The subject was never talked of again and Sarah made a determined effort to pull herself out of her self-defeating mood. She spent more time with Velvet who helped her with Arizona's training. Velvet gave her many tips and once Sarah asked her why she wouldn't ever ride him. 'Just once,' she said. 'Just to please me.'

'No.'

'But why not?'

'Oh, a variety of reasons. I live my riding life at second-hand now, through you.'

Sarah's dedication was now being rewarded. She and Arizona had a brilliant season, collecting honours in all the events they had entered for, enhancing their reputation. Tipped as being on the short list for the British team for the next Olympics, Sarah scanned every item in the newspapers, awaited the postman's daily visit with crossed fingers, and willed the telephone to ring.

The call, when it came, was typical of Johnson's personality.

'Why have you been avoiding me?' was his opening remark.

'I haven't.'

'Never call me, write to me.'

'Well, I would have done . . .'

'How's that horse of yours?'

'Fine. Never better.'

'Just as well because he's been picked for the Olympics.'

'Really? You're not kidding, are you? You wouldn't joke?'

'I don't know what kidding means and you'll remember that my jokes are few and far between. Now listen, since we want to take your horse I suppose we'd better take you, too. How does that sound?'

'It sounds fantastic!'

'Good. Well, you'll get the official letter tomorrow, telling you what to do, where to go and all that. Have to dress up for this one, you know. We'll all be getting together soon.'

'Is Beth coming, has she been chosen too?'

'Yes. Beth, Roger, Mike, Howard and you. The old gang in fact. Let's hope we have better luck than Ledyard. Right. That's all then, don't want to waste any more money on this call. I shall see you soon enough.'

The next few weeks passed in a haze of excitement. There were fittings for the official British uniforms, medical examinations, interviews, a press conference, veterinary inspections, passports and visas to be obtained, in addition to a heavy work schedule that Johnson insisted upon. They went back to the training establishment at Windsor for the final weeks before leaving, and if the programme had been demanding for Ledyard it was nothing compared to Johnson's Olympic preparations. He wanted the adrenalin to be flowing non-stop through both horses and riders. The team accepted the challenge, for there is always something uniquely special about the build-up to the Olympic Games. In direct contrast to Ledyard everything seemed to go smoothly. None of the horses got sick or were injured and such was Johnson's personality that he infused the team with his own total disregard for the possibility of failure. He schooled them in the Rules and Regulations for the Games until they knew them by heart.

'There's no room for error, no time for second thoughts,' he kept repeating. 'Know them like you know your ten times tables, so that they become second nature to you.'

The heart of the Olympic Equestrian Three-Day Event is, of course the cross-country speed and endurance test. Each horse is required to carry a minimum weight of 165 pounds and the test is made up of four stages. The first is the roads and tracks, some two to four miles, designed to warm up horse and rider. It must be accomplished at an average speed of nine miles an hour. The second phase is the steeplechase and this has to be ridden at a much faster pace – an average of twenty-six miles an hour, with penalty points all the way. If the rider doesn't complete within the time limit, he or she is eliminated. Three refusals at any obstacle also constitutes an automatic elimination.

In the Olympics there is no respite. Immediately following the steeplechase, the competitors must attempt a further six to ten miles of roads and tracks over varied terrain. At the end of this they get a ten-minute break while the official veterinary surgeons examine each horse and determine whether it is fit enough to continue. If so, the competitors take off for the toughest phase of all, a course which, over another four to five miles accommodates some thirty or forty really formidable obstacles: vertical fences, spread fences, ditches, banks, drops, water jumps, to be taken at an average speed of twenty-one miles an hour. This marathon is undertaken after the previous day's tension in the more formal dressage ring, and before the stadium jumping on the third consecutive day. It is truly the supreme test of man and animal, a test of stamina, courage, endurance and personality. It is the Olympics.

TEN

These particular Olympic Games were being held in a mid-European country behind the Iron Curtain and, with memories of the Munich tragedy still in everybody's minds, all the contestants were told to expect the tightest security precautions. They were warned they would be virtual prisoners within the limits of the Olympic Village that had been specially constructed by the host country, surrounded by heavily armed guards and electronic warning systems. Any contestant found in violation of the security regulations would be immediately eliminated and sent home.

Final preparations being completed, the British contingent left Heathrow Airport in time to become acclimatized to the foreign location. They wore smart and specially designed outfits and were, of course, subjected to close scrutiny by the news media. Television cameras and the Press were were out in force and because at eighteen she was the youngest competitor, particular attention was paid to Sarah. She found herself surrounded by a battery of cameras.

'How d'you feel being the baby of the team?' the television interviewer asked.

'Sort of not here,' Sarah answered with total honesty.

'Of course, as some viewers may be aware, riding is in your blood. Didn't I see your famous aunt around here?'

'Yes.'

The cameras switched to where Velvet and John were waiting with other relatives and well-wishers in the departure lounge.

'Sarah's aunt is Velvet Brown,' the interviewer explained. 'That's your middle name, too, isn't it? Well, you know what they called your aunt when she won the Grand National ... National Velvet. Maybe we should start calling you International Velvet?'

'Bit early for that,' Sarah said. She was half obscured by an enormous bouquet a fan had just thrust into her arms.

'Are you going to bring us back a gold?'

'We're going to try.'

'Well, I'm sure all our viewers at home join me in wishing you and the rest of the British team every success. We shall be covering all the main events live via satellite from the Olympic stadium and in the meantime it's good luck to Sarah Brown.'

'Thank you.' Sarah escaped thankfully and made her way back to Velvet and John.

'You must watch tonight – they mentioned you,' she told them.

'I hope you gave my book a plug,' said John.

'Oh no – I didn't think of ...'

'Only kidding.'

Velvet put her arms round Sarah.

'Darling, take great care of yourself.'

' 'Course I will.'

'Don't ... well, don't take any risks.'

'Listen who's talking!'

'We shall miss you.'

'I wish you were coming,' Sarah said.

'You don't wish it any more than us,' Velvet answered. She and John had discussed the matter endlessly, but the cost of the trip was beyond them and they had spent their last spare penny ensuring that Sarah had everything she wanted.

They watched from the roof of the departure building as the 'plane took off, waving long after it had become a small speck climbing into heavy clouds.

'Well, she made it,' Velvet said.

'Yes,' John said and Velvet noticed he had tears in his eyes.

Warnings about the security had not been exaggerated, and for the first day or so after their arrival Sarah and the team felt that they had been taken prisoner. They could hardly walk more than a few yards without being challenged, but gradually as the guards became more familiar with the various competitors, the atmosphere relaxed. The specially constructed Village for the Games was more like a futuristic city. Flags of all nations flew from a hundred flagpoles and the directional signs were written in a score of languages. Everybody was very friendly and the language barriers were soon overcome. Encircled by barbed wire, guard dogs and security police were some thousands of young people, all in the peak of physical condition, strangers to each other, yet all consumed by the common dedication. They were all conscious that few would leave the Village triumphant, for only the minority achieve fame, and yet, isolated from the world of politics and envy, class divisions and religious differences, bonded together by camaraderie, they achieved that rare equality of fellowship which eludes the rest of the world. They were in competition with each other, they were determined to make no concessions on the field of endeavour, but away from the arena they found their differences were few.

Sarah and the rest of the British contingent were immediately plunged into the final training schedule. Having given the horses time to settle in to their new quarters, Johnson insisted that there would be no let-up from his predetermined plan. Although the horses themselves never see any of the jumps before the event, the riders are allowed to walk the course and take stock of the problems they have to face.

Johnson led his team out on foot the moment permission had been given and it soon became obvious that what they were up against was truly an Olympic test. The course had been designed with great skill to ensure that whoever won the gold medal would have been tested to the limits.

'I don't want to frighten anybody,' Johnson said after they had returned from the walkabout, 'but that's the toughest course I've ever seen. Wouldn't you agree, Roger?'

'No question.'

'However, it's the same for everybody. No favours asked or given, and whatever the outcome, win or lose, the fact is you all made it here, and that's a prize in itself.'

He paused and rubbed his nose. 'As you know, I'm a noted sentimentalist, given to emotional outbursts . . . but I am proud of you all. I think I did a terrific job with some lousy material. And if you let me down, you can walk home . . .'

He seemed embarrassed by even this mild and muted compliment, as Sarah and the others agreed after he had left them alone.

'Poor old Johnson,' Mike said. 'I wonder how he ever managed to propose to his wives.'

'Probably got his horse to do it,' Howard said.

They were only too aware that Johnson had still to pick the team, and that there was little to choose between any of the horses. Whatever their secret hopes were, when they were together they all deliberately avoided the subject. Sarah forced herself to think of other things, but at night when sleep did not come easily, she willed herself to expect the worst. That was the advice Velvet had given. 'If you go in thinking, well it's not going to be me, then you can't lose either way,' Velvet had said. It was easier said than done, however.

Sarah was alone in the small room she shared with Beth on the fourth floor of one of the dormitory buildings the evening before the opening of the Games. She was studying the book of Rules for the hundredth time and didn't hear Beth come in.

'Oh, hi! I'll set your hair as soon as I've finished this once again,' she said. 'I hadn't forgotten.'

'No panic,' Beth said.

Something in her voice made Sarah look up sharply.

'What's the matter?'

'Johnson's announcing the team at six o'clock, but he told me first, which was nice of him.'

Sarah waited. 'You're riding, I'm not,' Beth said. It was a difficult moment. Sarah's natural elation fought with her sympathy.

'Oh, Beth, I'm sorry. Really. I'm not just saying that.'

'Why be sorry. Had to be somebody. As the understudy said, don't break a leg before the first night.'

'You mean *do* break a leg.'

'No, I'm really pleased for you. Really. You don't have to feel badly. I'm not crying.' Then her face suddenly dissolved. 'Yes, I am. I am crying, but don't take any notice, because it's nothing to do with you. Just reaction. So don't say anything, I mean don't be nice to me or anything . . . I'll get over it, only I'd rather get over it in my own way.'

Sarah nodded. 'Okay. Well, I'll come back and do your hair.'

She left the room quietly, but the moment she was downstairs in the compound she could no longer contain herself. She ran through the crowds of athletes, not knowing or caring where she was running to but simply running for the sheer joy of being alive. She ran straight into the arms of Scott Saunders as it happened, Fate being kinder than we imagine.

'Look who's here,' he said. 'Miss Brown from Cave Creek, or maybe I should say Miss International Velvet Brown. Did you see the papers?'

Sarah made a grimace. 'Yeah. Nauseating.'

'Oh, I don't know. I thought it was cute. Well, you look happy.'

'I am, I am! I got chosen, they picked me! I'm riding this time.'

'Congratulations. Can I buy you a Coke to celebrate?'

'Oh yes.'

They walked across the bridge which spanned the artificial lake towards one of the many restaurants.

''Course you realize I shouldn't fraternize with the enemy,' Scott said. 'But I guess this is a special occasion.'

'Everything's special, everything's perfect!'

'Careful! For all you know I might spike your drink.'

He took her arm as they threaded their way through the crowd.

She rang home that night.

'Are you all right?' was Velvet's immediate question the moment she picked up the phone.

'Yes, I'm fine. I've been chosen.'

'What? It's such a bad line. Say that again.'

'I've been chosen, Johnson picked me for the team.'

Velvet dropped the phone in her excitement.

'Darling, that's fantastic! Just . . . oh, I'm so thrilled for you. We shall be watching, they're showing a lot of it live on television.'

'That's a laugh,' Sarah said. 'I don't think I'll *be* alive, I'm so scared it's not true. I just wish you were here.'

'Well, we do too . . . Talk to John before your money runs out.'

'Hello, young Brown,' John said. 'Listen, you know me, I don't know one end of a horse from the other, but I know you're going to win. I've got money on it.'

'Not too much, I hope . . . but whatever the – whatever happens, I'll never forget what you both did to get me here. I love you both, and I love dear old Jack Delavie, too.'

Velvet and John were both sharing the earpiece by now.

'He's got quite a following,' Sarah continued. 'Over here, I mean, which'll give you some idea of the company I'm keeping. Most of them are okay, though . . . especially one.'

'What's that mean?'

But before she could answer the operator had cut in to announce that her time was up.

'That's it. Bye . . .'

'Good luck, darling,' Velvet shouted. 'All our love.'

The line went dead.

'Ah! wilderness,' John quoted. 'What it is to be young.'

'Heaven,' Velvet said, reaching for the Kleenex. 'That's what it is.'

Sarah's last call that night was a visit to the stables. She showed her security pass to the guards and walked down the line of stables, all in pristine order, to where Arizona awaited her in his stall. He had been rugged up for the night in his smart blue blanket.

'You posh old thing,' Sarah said. 'Look at you, all done up. Tomorrow's the day, you know. You don't care, do you?' She kissed his nose. 'I know you'll be all right.' Then, in a whisper, 'Just take care of me.'

She caught the coach back to the Olympic Village. Sitting in one corner of the rear seat was a young girl wearing a track suit with the Swedish emblem on it. She was crying. Sarah sat beside her and put her arm round her.

'What's wrong?'

'All over,' the girl said. Sarah gave her a handkerchief. 'Thank you.'

'What happened?'

'Is all over. I go back tomorrow. Sweden.'

'You mean you've been told to go home?'

The girl shook her head. 'No, is not that. Just is over. Eliminated. Three years I train, running, you know. Three years, every day training. Then today I run and nothing. Everybody run faster. So, finish. Is all over.'

She cried again and was still crying as they walked together in silence after the coach had dropped them at the entrance to the Village.

'You run?' the Swedish girl asked.

'No. I ride. Tomorrow.'

'Well, good luck.' She gave Sarah her handkerchief back.

Sarah watched her disappear into the Swedish block. For the first time in her life she suddenly realized what was at stake. That girl was like me, she thought. Training all those years, thinking of nothing else, doing nothing else, wanting nothing else. Then getting here, believing you're the best, that you've got a chance, and then finding out that your best is nothing compared to the others, all of whom have gone through the same thing, prepared in the same way, suffered the same agonies. You go out there in the arena, with the flags flying and the crowd roaring and you have one chance. The starter's pistol fires and you run until your heart feels it's going to burst . . . or you ride for dear life . . . and you come nowhere.

She stopped on the staircase leading up to her floor and rested her head against the cold metal of the stair-rail. The security guard standing on the next landing looked at her curiously.

'Please God' Sarah thought, 'let me do better than that. Don't let it all disappear at the first jump.'

The guard took a step down towards her. She recovered and smiled at him. He looked puzzled.

'Do you ever get lonely?' she asked.

'Oh, yes. Thank you.'

She realized that he didn't speak English, that he hadn't understood.

'Goodnight,' she said.

He touched his cap and smiled as she passed.

That night she had a dream. She saw Arizona racing, but the figure riding him seemed strange, and all the jumps kept receding. Towards the end of her dream the rider turned and waved, and it wasn't her face under the helmet, it was the face of the young Swedish girl.

ELEVEN

It rained all that night, and reports came back that conditions for the Dressage Test were likely to be heavy going.

'That's two in a row,' Roger said. 'First Ledyard and now this.'

'Still, same for everybody,' Mike volunteered.

'Yes, but the point is dressage isn't our strongest element and we need all the help we can get.'

They were all in the stable area helping the grooms make last-minute touches, every horse looking superb. They polished each other's boots, adjusted saddlery a fraction, oiled their horses' hooves, brushed their own jackets – occupying themselves as the minutes ticked away.

Johnson brought back early reports of the other competitors and the general opinion amongst the riders and officials was that it was going to be a difficult day. The sun was out now, but scarcely hot enough to dry out the sodden turf, and memories of Ledyard came crowding back. Although the dressage scoring is the least important of the three separate components of Combined Training, a bad dressage score can make the difference between victory and defeat by the end of the event. This is especially true of the Olympics where the general standard of riding is so high that sometimes only fractions of a point separate the leaders.

Sarah had been nominated to ride last for the British Team and was feeling too nervous to watch the others before her turn came. She remained in the exercise area until officials warned her to take her position. The crowd was large, but since the equestrian events take place away from the main stadium, it was not as large as she had imagined. Nevertheless she felt dwarfed as she urged Arizona into the dressage rectangle and took him down the centre line to make her stop in front of the judges' boxes. There were three of them, but she was unable to focus on them as she dipped her head towards the principal judge who stood and acknowledged her salute with a bow.

She had gained a feel of the soggy ground the moment she entered and now, as she took Arizona into the first movement of the complicated test, she felt his slight hesitation. She knew that her tension was being communicated to the horse and she willed herself to concentrate on the patterns of the dressage and nothing else. She could hear the echo of Johnson's voice, all those shouted instructions from the past, and now in the uncanny silence of the actual thing she longed for the sound of his sarcastic, comforting voice. But all she heard was the flop of Arizona's feet as he plucked them out of the wet turf, sounds magnified out of all proportion. Sit upright, she told herself, back straight, look ahead, hands still. She crisscrossed the rectangle, going from one alphabet marker to the next as though by instinct, while every nerve in her body tightened. Relax your hands, she told herself. You're gripping too hard, they notice that, they notice everything. Now, turn him. Now! Arizona responded, more sure-footed now, becoming, perhaps, a shade too confident. Sarah completed the half figure-of-eight, suddenly blinded as she turned into the sun. She felt she had been out there for hours and as she passed the judges' boxes yet again she fancied they were shaking their heads. Don't look, she told herself. Don't do anything, concentrate, concentrate, concentrate. The faces of the spectators were a blur behind the banks of specially planted flowers that surrounded the area.

Then it was over. She came to a halt after the last movement, brought her head up then down again for her salute to the judges. This time the principal judge did not get to his feet, but merely acknowledged the end of her test with the slightest of nods before consulting with one of his companions.

The gate at the far end of the rectangle was opened for her and the uniformed official saluted as she and Arizona made their exit. He reared as the wave of applause reached them, and she was forced to circle him before passing through into the unsaddling enclosure. She was just conscious of the next competitor going past her to take up his position and it wasn't until some time later that she registered that the rider had been Scott.

Johnson and other members of the British team crowded round her as her feet touched the ground.

'Well done,' Johnson said. 'I know what it's like out there and you managed very well.'

'I couldn't think straight.'

'No, one never can.'

'Did I look nervous?'

'A little, at the beginning, but you recovered all right. Not textbook perhaps, but as good as I could have hoped for.'

He left her then to study the opposition and compare the scores. Sarah was conscious of an overwhelming sense of anti-climax. She made sure that Arizona was given his share of compliments, then handed him over to her grooms and went and sat at the back of the refreshment tent. It was the first time she had ever experienced a loss of nerve.

At the end of the first day the British were placed seventh. 'No cause for celebration,' Johnson said, reverting to his familiar blunt manner. 'Post-mortems are for the dead. West Germany, the Australians and the Canadians all have the edge on us, but it's nothing we can't make up if we go well tomorrow.'

He turned to Roger. 'I want you to go over tomorrow's timings until you know them like the Lord's Prayer.'

Roger nodded agreement.

'Then *say* the Lord's Prayer.'

The rains held off that night and the following morning, the morning of the Cross-Country, the sky was overcast but bright with a keen wind that kept the flags stiff.

Carrying out Johnson's instructions Sarah and the other members of the team had walked the course twice. 'Once is not enough,' Johnson had said, 'and three times is dangerous. Over-familiarity with anything leads to complacency. You want just enough knowledge to be aware of what you're in for, and don't ever forget your horse is seeing it all for the first time, so you've got to think for him.'

Sarah had tried to mentally photograph the most difficult parts of the course, but just as an actor finds in the theatre, a dress-rehearsal is vastly different to the real thing in front of an audience. When they had walked the course they had it to themselves, now the countryside was dotted with clusters of spectators – there were colours everywhere instead of an uninterrupted vista of green. There was excitement in the air, the hum of voices, officials darting about as fussy and as nervous as some of the competitors, hordes of cameramen, television crews, all the paraphernalia that the world's media bring to the Olympics – sniffing around the perimeters of danger like trufflehounds, for the cross-country equestrian event is one of the few sports in the Olympic Games that embraces the possibility of a fatal accident.

Sarah went to the stables early to check that Arizona was fit and well and then left him undisturbed for the rest of the morning. As she was riding last for the Team it meant she was not due to run until fairly early in the afternoon. During the long wait she did her best to emulate Arizona and relax but she could not remain unoccupied. Apart from keeping up to date with the progress of all the early riders on the cross-country she occupied herself by having Beth test her memory of every twist and turn of the course and on her timings. Like most of the riders she wore two watches, a normal one and a stop watch.

Having been given the preliminary warning by one of the stewards she walked Arizona around for fifteen minutes. She came into the start as quietly as possible and throughout the roads and tracks concentrated on saving Arizona unnecessary exertion, dividing her time into periods of cantering and walking. Johnson's training and her own preparations paid off and she arrived at the start of the steeplechase course with two minutes in hand and without having incurred any penalty points. It was a good beginning to the day, and she used the time to tighten the girths.

She set off fast, keeping Arizona on the bit, moving him along at a fair pace as she had been trained, and letting him jump at speed without checking his stride. Again, it went well for her and she let Arizona unwind his gallop as he came into Phase C and by the time he had slowed to a walk they had covered some part of the second half of the roads and tracks. The Olympic course had been devised with care and thought, giving the horses a reasonable distance before the cross-country.

Johnson had urged them all to try and arrive at the Box for the start of the cross-country with a couple of minutes to spare, thus giving themselves twelve minutes to rest instead of the statutory ten.

'They're the most valuable two minutes you'll ever get in eventing,' he said.

Sarah came into the Box at a trot to impress the examining panel, slipped out of the saddle and was immediately surrounded by a posse of British grooms. They unsaddled Arizona and started to sponge him down from head to tail with warm water while Sarah conferred with Johnson.

'Any obvious faults you know of?' was his first question.

Sarah shook her head as she sipped a glucose drink.

'Timing's spot on,' Johnson said. 'Don't get over-confident, but I think you've done remarkably so far. How's Arizona behaving himself?'

'Enjoying every minute. I think he hated the dressage.'

They moved to where the horse was being towelled down. Two of the grooms were greasing his legs thickly from body to hoof, everybody working quietly and efficiently in the manner of a motor-racing pit crew. Johnson glanced at his watch.

'Four minutes,' he said.

They completed their grooming and saddled Arizona again. By the time Sarah mounted again all their good work had paid off and Arizona was no longer blowing.

The Starter began his count-down and Sarah moved Arizona into the starting box. It was only then that Johnson told her the bad news.

'Look, it's not confirmed yet, but it seems pretty certain that Roger has had to pull out. So remember our talk at

Ledyard. I know you'll do your best, but ride to get round, ride for the team. Good luck.'

She had no time to question him, for at that moment the Starter signalled her to go and she urged Arizona forward into a strong, relentless canter.

There were many spectators following her with special interest, for not only was she the youngest rider in the Games, but she also rode with a verve that some of the others lacked – her slight body poised over Arizona's centre of gravity, streamlined to cut down the wind drag. The British team rode in white sweat shirts with black silks over their helmets; this and Arizona's breast plate made them easy to spot and the crowd responded at every jump. Sarah didn't hear the applause in her wake: all she was conscious of was the steady, thudding rhythm of Arizona beneath her. He was jumping big at the early obstacles and it took all her strength to hold him sufficiently in check. 'Give him freedom,' Johnson had said, 'but never let him think you're not the boss.'

Oh, it was so easy, she thought, so easy to accept advice, so hard to act on it during the real thing. There were long distances between some of the jumps, the course taking many twists and turns. Arizona made a good approach to the water jump, although water was never his favourite obstacle, but partially straddled the bar. Sarah was thrown forward by the impact as the horse caught his hind legs on the bar, but she kept her head, picked up the reins and made a quick recovery. Arizona was balanced and going again and jumped out of the water and up the bank with confidence. They continued on their way, Sarah feeling she was lucky to have escaped from what had seemed, seconds before, certain disaster.

Arizona took the next two fences well, but she could sense that he was starting to get tired. They were roughly at the half-way mark and a quick glance at her stop-watch showed that they were making good time. She heard the echo of Johnson's words: 'Don't get over-confident.'

They came out of trees into strong light, the sun having just burst through a large bank of cloud, and for a moment or two Sarah was blinded. Her memory of the next obstacle blurred and she took it badly. Arizona momentarily lost his stride and was awkwardly positioned to take the following jump. They came down a grassy bank and she steered him to one side of the dip beyond the grass, then urged him again to make the effort up the bank on the other side, to the gigantic brush fence. It seemed to tower over them as they came into it, a black mass, with the sun directly ahead, and Arizona faltered. Sarah lost a stirrup and as Arizona refused she was flung to one side and thudded into the middle of the brush. She fell awkwardly, clear of the horse, but on to her left shoulder. She was conscious of a sudden searing pain which blotted out sky and grass into a distorted series of images, as though a reflection had suddenly shattered.

Arizona ran to one side of the fence and officials headed him off and retrieved him. Scarcely conscious of what she was doing Sarah got to her feet again. The rules allowed her to accept help to remount and she was quickly back in the saddle, but as she picked up the reins with her left hand the pain returned. She brought Arizona round and trotted him back down the slope and repositioned him for the second attempt. She knew that she had incurred twenty penalty points for the refusal and another sixty for the fall. 'Don't refuse again,' she prayed. 'Please, don't refuse again.' She had the feeling that if she didn't get over clean at the second attempt the pain would take over. She urged Arizona up the slope – the brush fence loomed again, and then she felt the swish of it beneath her, and she was sailing over. 'Oh, you darling,' she shouted, 'you darling, you did it!' and heard the applause from the crowd in their wake for the first time.

Then the pain in her shoulder came back in great waves, but it seemed strangely remote as though it was all happening to somebody else. She couldn't connect it with what she was doing. It was like pain felt in a dream. She had heard other riders talk about the same thing, how they had ridden with broken ribs, concussed, with badly torn muscles and yet not been conscious of the extent of the injuries until the round had been completed. She took the next jump and the next, and although she was aware that she was taking part, her actions were reflexes, and it was Arizona who was in control. The scenery and the spectators rushed by like speeded-up film – flashes of colour, snatches of noise. Another jump ahead, pulling her towards it, then over, and down on the other side, the impact jarring her injured shoulder, but no time to think, no time to feel sorry for herself, because Arizona was striding on and there was another obstacle on the horizon. She saw everything as though through the wrong end of a telescope. Now they were sailing through the air again, over the coffin jump, down, up again, into the dip and taking the second set of rails, then racing downhill for a stretch, a long curving approach through birch trees leading to the log pile. Over that. Only four more to go, or was it five? She had a moment of total panic, thinking that her memory of the course had been erased and that she had taken a wrong turn and ruined everything. What should come next? She dimly recalling a warning from Johnson: 'The last ones will fool you. You'll think you're home and dry because they look easy, and in fact they are a lot simpler than some of the earlier jumps, but don't forget your horse will be tired, you'll be tired, mentally and physically, prone to errors.'

She held on. In front of her were three sleeper-faced upward leaps. She knew she had to make Arizona take them at speed. Now she had no feeling at all in her arm. As though sensing her pain Arizona summoned a last reserve of strength and took the leaps without breaking stride. They looked down on the home stretch from the other side. Spectators were massed all the way to the finish and suddenly there was the end in sight, and she made for it, putting her head down and praying that she could last.

They crossed the electronic finishing line and somehow she pulled Arizona round and headed him for the un-saddling enclosure. She knew she could expect no help until she had weighed in again. She slipped from Arizona's back and was vaguely conscious of Beth, Tim and Johnson coming forward with smiles on their faces. Then the dragging weight of the saddle cradled in her one good arm. She managed to get onto the scales and off again before the ground began to swim away. She felt the saddle slipping from her grasp and a rush of green coming up to meet her and then there was nothing – she slipped into a noisy void. The world was suddenly still and merciful.

She was rushed by ambulance to the specially constructed Olympic hospital and immediately attended to by the British team surgeon. He diagnosed a dislocated shoulder and mild concussion. The effort of riding on after the fall had torn the muscles and although the shoulder was quickly put back into position she awoke to more pain. Johnson and the doctor were conferring at the end of her bed and she could tell by their faces that they felt her to be a lost cause.

'How's Arizona?' she whispered.

'He's fine.'

143

'How did we do?'

'Not bad,' Johnson said. 'Not bad at all for a cowboy. In fact it was a remarkable piece of riding . . . Mike and Howard also had good rounds.'

'And Roger?'

'Roger had to withdraw.'

The implications of what Johnson had just said began to sink in. She tried to sit up in bed.

'Now just take it easy, young lady,' the doctor said. 'You're not going anywhere for the time being. Just rest.'

Sarah ignored him. 'So I have to ride tomorrow,' she told Johnson. 'I mean, are we still in there with a chance?'

'Yes. In fact we're in second place for the team medal.'

'Who's first?'

'The Americans. They had no eliminations. The West Germans are lying a close third to us and the Australians are only two points behind them.'

'There must have been quite a shake-up then?'

Johnson nodded. 'The cross-country really shuffled the pack. But that doesn't solve our problem, Miss Brown.'

The sudden, mock formality emphasized his concern.

'I'll be all right,' Sarah said. 'Don't worry.'

'You'll be all right if the doctor says you're all right. You're not allowed pain-killers, you know.'

'I know. Haven't got any pain.'

'Tell that to the marines. You forget I took a few spills in my time, and I know what a dislocated shoulder feels like.'

'I'm fine, I tell you. The person I'm sorry for is poor Roger. What happened to him?'

'His horse slipped a tendon.'

'Did they . . .?'

'No. Tim thinks he can save him, but I doubt whether he'll ever event again.'

'Well, that settles it, doesn't it?"

'Sarah,' Johnson said. 'The doctor will take the decision. Not you, not me. And he's not going to say anything now. You'll be examined again in the morning.'

Sarah smiled at them both. 'Look at your faces,' she said. 'You're worrying about nothing.'

She swung her legs over the side of the hospital bed in a show of bravado and had to catch her breath at the stab of pain that the sudden movement produced.

'I don't have to stay here, do I?'

'No, you can go back to the Village,' the doctor said. 'But take it easy. I've strapped you up and I want you to stay strapped. Those muscles have taken a beating, you know.'

Mike was waiting in the corridor outside the ward and helped her back to the Village. As with Johnson, Sarah was determined to convince him that she felt all right, but it took an effort. Her legs seemed to lack any strength and her whole body ached. Thank God, she thought, that Velvet wasn't here. I wouldn't be able to fool her.

Sarah had forgotten that everything that happens at the Olympics is news. The BBC television cameras had been on the spot when she had her fall and the incident was given prominence in that night's coverage of the event. Velvet and John were both watching the programme when they heard Sarah's name mentioned: 'Hope is now centred on young Sarah Brown who rode Arizona Pie so brilliantly today,' the commentator said . . . and there she was on the screen. Then they saw her fall at the brush fence. 'Despite this, she remounted and finished the course and we're still awaiting news that she has been passed fit to compete in the final event.'

Before the commentator had finished Velvet had reached

145

for the phone and dialled the International Operator.

'Sarah? Are you all right? We just heard the news on the television.'

'Yes, truly, I'm fine.'

'Did you break anything?'

'No, I just pushed my shoulder about a bit.'

'Well, listen darling, please be sensible. You musn't ride if it's dangerous, nothing's worth that.'

'But if I don't ride, the whole team will be eliminated.'

'At least promise me you won't do anything stupid.'

'I promise.'

'See, I worry about you, we both do, and all I'm saying is, be careful . . .'

Sarah reassured her. The rest of the conversation left Velvet rather puzzled for she sensed that Sarah had somebody else in the room at her end and was anxious to finish the call. Her instincts were right, except that Sarah wasn't in a room but on the stairway of her dormitory block and the person with her was Scott Saunders. He had been on his way to enquire about her when they met on the stairway.

'You should be resting,' he said when she had replaced the receiver. She still had her shoulder strapped.

'Everybody says that. I'm putting you all on. Nothing serious. But it was real nice of you to come round . . . You had a great ride today.'

'I got lucky,' he said.

'I guess we both did.'

'What I came to say was, win or lose, I'll take you out to dinner tomorrow. Is that a date?'

She stared at him.

'Is it a date?'

'Yes,' she said. 'It's a date.'

He leaned in suddenly and kissed her.

'Get some rest,' he said. 'Goodnight.'

'Goodnight.'

She stood there on the stairway for a full minute after he had gone, then turned and ran back to her room, and for the first time since the accident she felt no pain.

Although she woke feeling very stiff the following morning she insisted on taking Arizona out for his early morning exercise before preparing him for the final veterinary inspection.

'What impresses me,' Mike said with his usual cynicism, 'is that they never give a damn what shape *we're* in.'

All three British horses passed the inspection and again the drama centred on Sarah. The team doctor re-examined her and his diagnosis was gloomy.

'Johnny, I still think it's very questionable whether she should ride. The shoulder's back in place, but obviously it's very tender and I doubt if she'll have more than fifty per cent use of that arm.'

'I want to ride,' Sarah insisted.

Johnson was pacing up and down.

'Don't let's argue, please!' Sarah went on. 'I *have* to ride, you know that. Arizona'll get me over . . . and I'm not being brave, I just know it'll be all right.'

'I have to weigh up the risks,' Johnson said.

'It'd be different if you had to talk me into it.'

'The doctor agrees with me.'

'What? What did he say?' She turned on the doctor. 'What did you say? You said fifty per cent use. You didn't say I couldn't ride.'

'I said it was questionable whether you should.'

'Well, what can happen? All that can happen is that I have to pull out. I know I can't get the medal for me, I know that. But the team still have a chance. So let me go in and take the first jump. It'll either work or it won't and if it doesn't we're no worse off. Mike, you say something.'

'Sarah, I'm not a doctor,' Mike answered.

'But you want me to ride, don't you?'

'I don't want you to kill yourself, or Arizona.'

An official ducked under the flap of the British tent.

'Excuse me, Captain Johnson, but you are cutting it very fine, you know.'

'Yes, I know.'

'There's only five minutes left before the list is closed. Have you decided yet?'

'Tell him!' Sarah pleaded.

Johnson stared at her, then walked outside the tent and stood with his back to them. They waited. The official glanced at his watch again. Sarah held Mike's hand. Then Johnson turned.

'All three members of the British team will be riding,' he said.

'Oh, thank you, thank you,' Sarah said and went to kiss him.

'Save that for when it's all over. Right! Howard and Mike . . . Sarah is riding last for the team anyway, so if you both get clear rounds she can go, but if we haven't got a prayer by the time she's called, I'll scratch her. Understood?'

'Understood,' both men said.

Johnson looked long and hard at Sarah.

'Fair?'

She nodded.

The show-jumping section of the Three-Day Event is not so much a test of the horse's ability as a jumper, but more a searching examination of his character. By professional show-jumping standards, the fences for a Three-Day Event are tame stuff, but they have to be faced after the gruelling cross-country of the preceding day. Horses and riders have survived the dressage and the speed and endurance tests, and must now come to terms with the tensions of the arena.

The starting scores between the leaders that day were so close that Johnson's analysis was correct. Without clear rounds from both Mike and Howard, the question of Sarah's participation was academic. In addition, even if all three members of the British team went clear that still wouldn't be sufficient to capture the team gold medal unless their leading rivals collected some faults. It promised, as the BBC commentator kept repeating in his excitement, to be a real cliff-hanger.

Back in Mothecombe Velvet and John were more on edge than anybody in the arena. They had invited some of the local villagers to share what they hoped would be a great celebration. News that Sarah had passed the fitness test had already been given and the entire final event was being televised live via satellite. John had the champagne on ice and before the first rider entered the arena he had already chained-smoked his way through a whole packet of twenty.

'You're going to be in intensive care before Sarah comes on,' Velvet said.

'I can't help it.'

Velvet explained the complicated method of scoring as best she could to some of their guests.

'Does it look a difficult course to you?' asked George, the local policeman.

'They're all difficult, George.'

'Well, I hope Miss Sarah can hang on,' Alice said.

'Oh, I've got my fingers crossed,' Velvet said. 'I may never get them uncrossed. I just hope she's all right.'

At that moment there was a picture of Sarah on their screen. She looked calm enough but they could see that she had a black bandage holding her injured arm strapped to her body.

'I presume they've given her a pain-killer,' John remarked.

'Not allowed.'

'Nothing?'

'Not even an aspirin. I've known people ride with broken ribs and they still don't get anything.'

'I'll stick to writing.'

The first horse, one of the German team, came into the arena. The cameras panned over the packed rows of spectators from all nations, suddenly hushed now as the German rider commenced his round.

'Germany, placed third at the start of this, the final event,' the commentator said. 'Still in with a chance and with four very fine horses.'

The German rider took the early fences with style, making it look easier than it was, and then perhaps relaxed slightly and undershot the water jump.

'Ten penalties,' Velvet shouted.

They watched as the rider recovered and galloped at the brick wall. His horse seemed to balk at the very last moment and the top of the wall went flying in all directions. This seemed to be the pattern for the next six or seven riders. They began well, but then a minor fault led to bigger and bigger errors and by the time Howard entered the arena no competitor had turned in a clear round.

Flying Scot was the most experienced horse the British team had, and from the first it looked as if the course held no problems for him. Jumping fluently and with zest, he cleared fence after fence without a mistake, and the huge crowd was silent as he approached the last, a big triple. The BBC commentator could not conceal his excitement: 'He's over the first . . . and the second, and, yes, yes, he's done it! And inside the time limit, so that's a clear round for Howard Purcell of Great Britain on Flying Scot.'

The first two American and Australian riders, strong contenders for the gold, also went clear, and then it was Mike's turn. Howard had briefed him on what he considered were the major problems and he felt calm and detached. 'I shall do it,' he thought. 'I shall do it because I have to do it, I have to give Sarah a chance. Ergo, I shall do it!'

He had determined to stay close to the fences, allowing his own confidence to flow through to his horse, and the ploy worked. Although he rapped a couple, they stayed up and he chalked up the second clear round for Great Britain.

As he left the arena to prolonged applause Mike searched for Sarah. She was waiting by the side of Arizona in the warm-up area; she hadn't dared watch Mike's round, but the volume of applause told its own story. She flung her one good arm round him as he dismounted.

'Save your energy,' Johnson said. 'Go on, I gave you my word. Just go in there and clinch it.'

'Do we still have a chance?'

'We have a chance,' Johnson said flatly.

While all this was going on behind the scenes and out of range of the television cameras, Velvet and John were hanging on to every word of the commentary.

'Well, the pressure's really on the Americans now. Scott Saunders, the American team captain, can't afford any penalty points if he's going to keep the heat on Sarah Brown.'

'What's that mean?' John said.

'Well, they haven't shown the scoreboard recently,' Velvet answered, 'but when we last saw it, just before Mike went clear, we'd moved up ahead of the Germans and the Australians.'

'So, tell me, tell me!'

'I'm trying. If Sarah drops more than ten points and this Scott character goes clear, then we've lost the gold. But I'm not sure. Don't ask me, just watch, we'll miss it.'

They watched as Scott entered the ring looking every inch a champion, his horse's head turning from side to side as Scott loosened him up. They took fence after fence in effortless style.

'Oh, hit something!' Velvet shouted at the screen.

'That's sporting of you,' John said.

'I can't help it.'

Scott was jumping faultlessly, and perhaps the easing of tension made him relax concentration for a few seconds. He seemed unaware that he was taking the course at a slow pace, never turning tight between jumps.

'I think he'll have time faults,' the commentator said. 'Unless he makes it up on the last two fences, I think he'll be just outside the limit. What a shame.'

'Oh, don't be so blessedly neutral,' Velvet said.

Scott took the triple, just touching the last bar, but it didn't topple. They waited until the cameras swung over to a shot of the official timing.

'Yes!' the commentator exclaimed. 'He got time faults. Well, that was certainly the last thing we expected from a rider of his experience. It just goes to show that nothing is for certain in the Olympics.'

John moved to the ice bucket where the champagne was waiting. 'Don't touch it!' Velvet said. 'It's bad luck.'

They stared at the screen and there, suddenly, just visible over the heads of the crowd in the foreground, was

Sarah on Arizona. '. . . looking very composed,' the commentator said.

There were no microphones near her otherwise the world audience might have heard what Sarah said when she bent to whisper in Arizona's ear. 'Listen, you,' she said. 'Don't do it for me, do it for your father. He won the Grand National, remember? And you've got to show him.'

She straightened up again and walked him through the gate and into the arena. There was no more advice to be had, no Johnson to listen to, she was alone. Trotting Arizona round in a wide circle she felt the tension build in her as she listened intently for the sound of the judges' bell – the signal that she might start her round. Arizona sensed her excitement and, handicapped as she was by her arm, she had difficulty in holding him back. 'Steady, boy, oh steady,' she prayed, knowing that if he were to cross the starting-line before the judges gave their permission, she would be disqualified. Then the bell shrilled and immediately she felt the familiar surge of adrenalin run through her body. She cantered him towards the first fence, breaking the electronic beam and starting the digital clock.

From the way Arizona took the jump she knew immediately that his appetite had not been dimmed by the experiences of the previous day. The pain in her arm vanished. Arizona's stride was smooth and rhythmic. He took the water high and wide. Jumping in copybook fashion, folding well and using his head and neck correctly, he treated every fence with respect. There was no sound from the packed audience. They cleared the seventh, eighth and ninth. The atmosphere was electric. Unless a last-minute tragedy occurred it was obvious to everybody watching that history was about to be made. Even some of those who had most to lose were willing this diminutive figure on the flying horse to win. They were aware of her injury, aware that the British team had only three riders, and that the elusive gold medal was within reach, just three fences away.

At home Velvet was no longer able to watch. She covered her eyes.

'She's over the square oxers,' the commentator said and even his professional voice had a break in it. 'Now there's just the triple and she's well ahead of the clock.'

Arizona met the last fence on a fluent, lengthening stride, taking off close to the first element. He cleared this and was over the second. Then time seemed to hang still, for Sarah, for those in the arena and for those at home. Arizona jumped again – an extravagant last demonstration of his ability – and they were over and through the finishing beam and the arena erupted.

'She's done it, she's done it, she's done it!' the BBC commentator shouted, casting his neutrality to the winds. 'Sarah Brown has done it for Great Britain! No jumping faults, no time faults. We shall have the official announcement in a few seconds, but I can tell you that is the gold medal, ladies and gentlemen.'

The whole stadium erupted as the placings were confirmed and flashed onto the electronic scoreboard.

GREAT BRITAIN	363.8
U.S.A.	365.8
AUSTRALIA	480.3

As Sarah came into the unsaddling enclosure she was surrounded by the whole British contingent, not only the equestrian team but athletes as well, for word had quickly spread that there was a real chance for the gold. She was almost dragged from Arizona by well-wishers. Beth was crying, even the usually unemotional Roger was distinctly misty-eyed, his own disappointments forgotten in the reflected glory of the moment. Mike and Howard, still sweating from their own rounds, converged on her from both sides in a united bear-hug. There was Tim and the team doctor and all the grooms, their faces shiny with pride, and Sarah suddenly realized what it meant to be part of a team, that nobody could do it alone, and that the sharing was more important than anything else. Johnson came up to her through the crush, his congratulations almost embarrassed, and she kissed him impulsively and saw his face redden.

'You've got to go out there again, you know, you three. Go and receive your medal!'

'Our medal,' Sarah said.

'Well, I'll let you keep it,' Johnson said.

Back home Velvet saw some of this as the television cameras moved in. John had opened the champagne and they were toasting each other, toasting Sarah, Arizona, the whole British team. They watched as Sarah, Mike and Howard, with Johnson and grooms leading the horses, walked back into the arena and mounted the presentation dais, taking the place of honour in the middle. Mike and Howard stood on either side of Sarah. The pageantry of the moment made Velvet start crying again. She saw the American team take their places and on the other side of Sarah, Mike and Howard, the Australians, in third place, completed the winning groups.

Girls in national costumes of the host country lined up with bouquets of flowers as the President of the Games and his entourage made their stately way down the steps from the VIP box. The medals were carried on cushions by three other young ladies.

'It's so beautifully staged,' Velvet said. 'I can't believe

Sarah's actually there, standing there. She did it! I mean she really did it.'

'Now just calm down otherwise you'll miss it,' John said.

By now the President was standing in front of the British team. He removed his hat, then took the gold medal from the cushion. Sarah bent forward so that he could place the medal round her neck and as she straightened again the sun caught it, flaring the television screen. The crowd rose to her and the President shook her hand and lingered to say his personal congratulations before turning to Howard and Mike. Various other officials followed him. There was a close-up of Sarah and now Velvet could see her fingering the medal, turning it to show the two boys. They kissed her.

Then the shot changed and it was the turn of Scott's team to receive their silver medal. Another roar from the crowd, and then another as the Australians were handed the bronze. Immediately the presentations had been completed, and with that impeccable timing that is the hallmark of the Games, the flags of the three victorious nations were hoisted, the Union Jack occupying the place of honour in the centre. And as it reached the top of the pole the band played 'God Save The Queen'.

Sarah felt Howard and Mike straighten to attention on either side of her, and it was only then that the enormity of the occasion overwhelmed her and she swayed slightly, and for a moment the world went black and she felt that she was going to faint. Mike's hand touched hers and his fingers tightened in her palm. The moment passed and she looked up at the flag, conscious of the weight of the medal around her neck.

On the television screen she looked a tiny figure, dwarfed by those around her. As the National Anthem finished the cameras zoomed out to show the entire arena and the roar of the crowd was like a thunder-clap. Sarah, Mike and Howard turned and raised their arms in triumphant salute to the far side of the arena. There, facing them on the massive scoreboard was the confirmation of all that had gone before – the taking part, the struggle, and the great joy of winning.

Sarah turned again, looking for Johnson. He stood alone, close to his horses, and he had taken off his hat for the Anthem and was still bare-headed. She willed him to look in her direction and finally he raised his eyes. She saw his mouth move, but there was no means of telling what he was saying to her, for the noise of the continuing applause swamped all, but he was smiling at her and she hoped she had at long last convinced him that in conquering she had also fought well.

TWELVE

Today and Tomorrow

It was late afternoon and for the second time that day Velvet walked alone along the edge of the sea. The sands were as smooth as freshly-laid concrete, glistening where the sun caught the surface moisture. Here and there the white backs of shells stranded by the receding tide, the occasional rock pool slimed with seaweed, pieces of bleached drift-wood, the handle of a child's spade sticking up at an angle like an ancient gravestone.

Velvet picked her way carefully, her footprints fading behind her as though her progress across the beach paralleled all that had gone before – the slate wiped clean.

Four days had slipped by since the consuming excitement of the victory celebrations. Four days of anti-climax, then anxiety when no word came from Sarah; puzzlement turning to worry and, since the arrival of the telegram, worry replaced by hurt. The sea calmed her. She turned and started to retrace her steps inland, hands thrust deep into the pockets of her red trenchcoat. Looking up she saw John coming across the sands to meet her. She walked a little further and then stood waiting for him.

'Don't tell me you're actually taking some exercise?' she said.

'Just being a messenger boy. This came for you. Special delivery.'

He held out a small package.

'What is it?'

'Darling, how should I know? I haven't opened it. It's addressed to you.'

She took it from him, suspicious.

'This isn't one of your awful jokes, is it?'

'No. Why should it be a joke?'

'Because I know you.'

She opened the package carefully. There was something inside, wrapped in tissue paper. She looked at John again, but his face was bland. Removing the tissue paper, she found a flat jewellery box. She pressed the catch and there was a folded piece of paper inside with her name written on it. A sudden gust of wind blew the paper to the sand as though on cue and she saw that the box contained an Olympic gold medal.

She stared at it for several seconds. John bent and retrieved the letter from the damp sand.

'Don't you want to read what came with it?'

Velvet shook her head. 'You read it.'

He unfolded the paper. 'I know there's more to winning than the prizes – you taught me that – but since you never got to keep yours, I'd like you to have this. Love always, Sarah.'

She was crying by now, she couldn't help herself. John put his arms around her and let her cry, then gently turned her round in the direction of the causeway.

'Oh, and by the way,' he said. 'It was hand-delivered.'

Velvet stared across the sands. Coming down the causeway slope were two figures, a tall young man and a girl dressed in white. And as she looked the girl rested a hand on the young man's shoulder while she removed her shoes. Then, carrying the shoes in one hand, the girl started to run barefooted across the beach.

'It's Sarah! You knew, you knew all the time!' Velvet said.

Sarah ran to her and they met and embraced like lovers at the end of a long war. Then Sarah turned and led the young man forward.

'Scott,' she said, 'I'd like you to meet my parents.'

The young man held out his hand and Velvet took it, but she couldn't see his face clearly for the tears in her eyes, and she was not crying for herself, she was crying for the agony of happiness, for what Sarah had said, for something she had never known before.